Carrion Colony

Richard King was born in 1968 and lives in Clunes, Victoria. His first novel, *Kindling Does for Firewood*, was the winner of the *Australian*/Vogel Literary Award.

CARRION COLONY

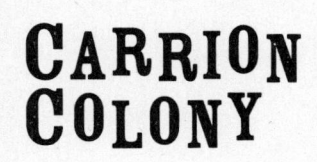

Richard King

First published in 2002

Copyright © Richard King 2002

All rights reserved. No part of this book may be reproduced or transmitted in any form or by any means, electronic or mechanical, including photocopying, recording or by any information storage and retrieval system, without prior permission in writing from the publisher. The *Australian Copyright Act 1968* (the Act) allows a maximum of one chapter or 10 per cent of this book, whichever is the greater, to be photocopied by any educational institution for its educational purposes provided that the educational institution (or body that administers it) has given a remuneration notice to Copyright Agency Limited (CAL) under the Act.

Australia Council for the Arts

This project has been assisted by the Commonwealth Government through the Australia Council, its arts funding and advisory body.

Allen & Unwin
83 Alexander Street
Crows Nest NSW 2065
Australia
Phone: (61 2) 8425 0100
Fax: (61 2) 9906 2218
Email: info@allenandunwin.com
Web: www.allenandunwin.com

National Library of Australia
Cataloguing-in-Publication entry:

King, Richard, 1968– .
  Carrion colony.

  ISBN 1 86508 760 2 (pbk.).

  1. Penal colonies—Australia—Fiction. 2. Australia—History—1788–1851—Fiction. I. Title.

A823.3

Text design by Simon Paterson
Set in 10/16 pt Goudy by Bookhouse, Sydney
Printed in Australia by McPherson's Printing Group

10 9 8 7 6 5 4 3 2 1

For my grandmother,
Jessie Magdalene Wakefield,
1908–1996

To walk into history is to be free at once, to be at large among people.

                    Elizabeth Bowen, *The House in Paris*, 1935

The historical sense involves a perception, not only of the pastness of the past, but of its presence.

      T. S. Eliot, *Tradition and the Individual Talent*, 1919

You know how it is, fellow historians—you look for a little patch not trod too hard by other footsteps, where maybe you can grow a few sweetpeas.

John Updike, *Memories of the Ford Administration*, 1992

CARRION COLONY

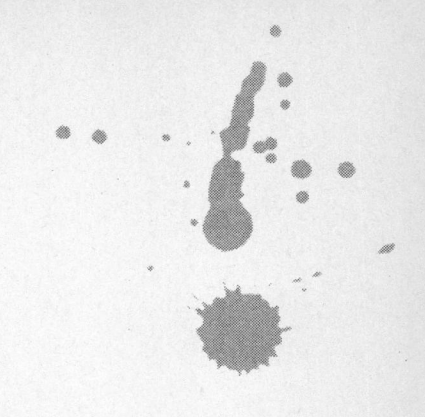

Epilogue

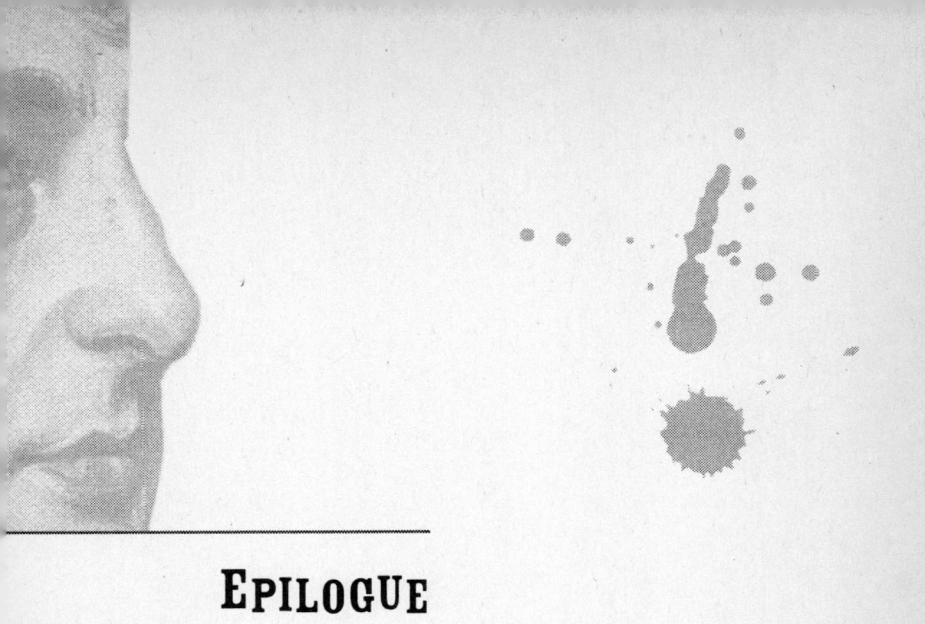

Several hundred years ago next Tuesday, the complete silence that shrouded that colony upon the hill was not the first thing the visiting soldiers noticed. They were aware of the unrelenting still, it compelled their attention, it demanded their consideration, it required an explanation, but it wasn't the first thing they were aware of. It was astonishing the absence of people in this village, with one exception there was not a soul to be seen. It was unnerving, distracting and commanded address but it wasn't the thing that commanded address the most. This place was haunted. There were the voices of dead souls about this land, there were cries of agony in the wind that compelled one's heart and compelled one's whole attention, but their voices were not nearly as compelling as that of the filthy old man in the fetid old clothes, wearing the Governor's hat, and sitting behind the pegboard table.

'You have made port in Her Majesty's Colony of Old & New Bridgeford under the Command of Governor John Dunnock. Please state your business.' He shrieked from the time that they set foot upon that shore until the time they reached his higgledy-piggledy table set far up and away upon the beach in the shade of the higgledy-piggledy tree.

'You have made port in Her Majesty's Colony of Old & New Bridgeford under the Command of Governor John Dunnock. Please state your business.' He repeated again and again until finally, to silence the poor fellow, one of their company said, 'Are You Not Of Good Sense Sir?'

The indignant and exasperated effrontery this provoked in the strange old lunatic did little to refute the merit of the inquiry, in fact it did much to suggest an answer.

'Can You Show Us To People We Can Talk To?'

'That's enough of that.' Said the Governor. 'I am John Dunnock, Governor of Old & New Bridgeford, here are some papers, here is a commission of Arthur's, here is a ledger, here a great something full of numbers and nothings. The old Governor is dead, I am his successor, my pardon was his last commission. You have made port in Her Majesty's Colony of Old & New Bridgeford under the Command of myself, John Dunnock. At once, see my hat and state your business.'

The soldiers' *business* was surrendering thirteen hundred convicts to the jurisdiction of the penal colony of New Bridgeford, established ten months prior, and a village of some nine hundred-say souls. Some of them were to make their homes here in this new land of New South Wales, some of them were to return to England on the ships. Neither group thought much of the place.

'You have made port...'

The soldiers fast decided that this here sure smacked aplenty of a matter for the Captain.

Captain Fratini looked at the vague and deranged fellow before him, wondered at the wisdom of leaving these thirteen hundred thieves, murderers and villains to the care of this frail old gentleman, whether it was witful to entrust to his command the seethe of rebellious soldiers, this intrigue of officers. Old Governor Storkbones coughed and then knocked his pen and inkwell from his table and then knocked over his table as he strove to retrieve the former.

Captain Fratini considered his options and was fast eager to strike a deal.

'You the Governor here?'

'You have made port in Her Majesty's...'

'Her Majesty's a him now. Are you as Governor of this colony able to accommodate an additional thirteen hundred prisoners, further troops, stock and feed?'

'Perhaps.'

'Fine.' Said Captain Fratini. He had just sailed over half the globe and more with these one thousand and three hundred convicts; he did not particularly feel like taking them on the journey back. The owner of the ships and the financiers required that he leave these convicts here, His Majesty's Administration of Gaols and Penal Settlements required that he leave these prisoners here, His Majesty's Royal Navy and the depleted provisions of his fleet required that he leave these thirteen hundred convicts here, if this mad old grubby bugger wanted them he was welcome to have them no questions asked. 'I have done my job.' Thought Captain Fratini. 'And if there's ever a problem with this situation, why I'll off to China and trade tea with the Yellowmen.'

He'd had enough with transporting *freight* for the English, it was a fucking disgrace, it made his soul vomit.

Governor Dunnock watched the new soldiers herd and scurry the new convicts here and there. He studied their faces; he checked their mien. He was shocked by the unknown stories and the unfamiliar character their frowns and glowers and blinded blinking suggested. He searched for a Young Collins or a Dear Lizzie or a Wee Robert, a Doctor Wilmot or a Corporal Beamish or an Astronomer Casey amongst their cunning company and he found only the foreign shoulder of some other person, the dishevelled hair and the alien scowls of a connivance of strangers.

Not a Naskin, not a Bridewell, not a Snivey or a Hook, no Collins, not a Lizzie or a Dear Wee Sweet Robert or the other lad, not one of the eight fellows who rowed the boat, they were all gone, dead, digested or cast to the wind.

This was a whole new lot of people.

He commanded a certain clutter of them to move more quickly between a certain point here and a certain point there, and they immediately obeyed.

He sat back in amazement.

He bid one person defer his travel and relate his name, crime and sentence. The fellow complied and had his hat in his hand the entire time. Governor Dunnock waved the man away and then giggled when the chap saluted.

'Good Lord.' Said Governor Dunnock. Governor Dunnock had found himself in that sad and unfortunate situation in life—some of us do—where he had on this earth not a lover nor a friend, no family or companions, not a mentor or an acolyte, not a master or an admirer. He hadn't received any personal letters or correspondence on these last ships from England—no bills to be signed or wills to be witnessed, not a love letter sealed with a kiss or a hateful threat penned in poisoned ink—but by God, he had received a chessboard.

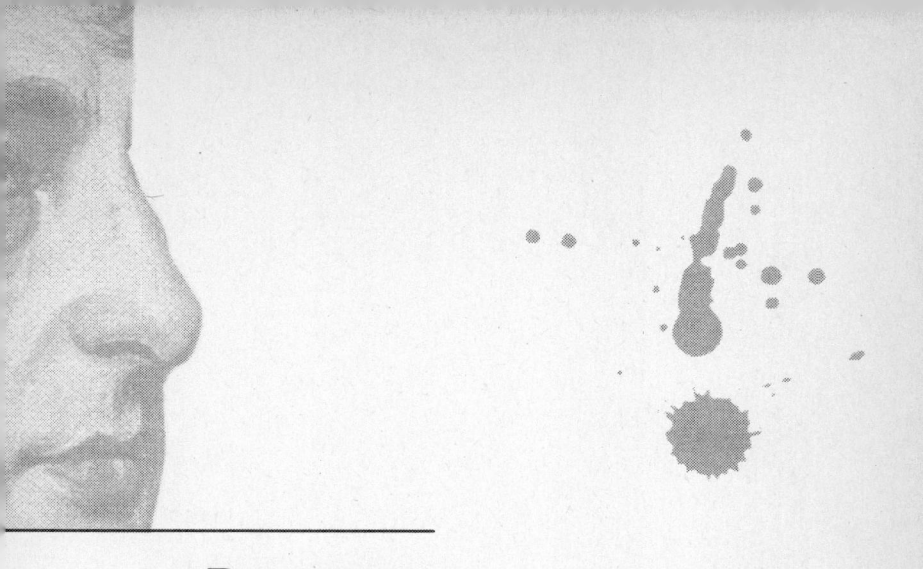

Prologue

Young Corporal Beamish did not like Wednesdays, he could barely abide and bear them; they made a bloody and buggeried mess, a bastard mess of his Tuesdays.

He did not, on Tuesdays, do a thing that could possibly bring him any joy or pleasure or abandon, because that same panacea, that same balm or elixir or intoxicant, would fuck with his guts the very next day. He would wake on a Wednesday morning free from hangover, grin or distemper, and for those few disoriented seconds wonder that surely any day that found him in such good spirits must prove to be a day of worth and opportunity indeed. Then he'd growl like a dog and with his fists pound the bedclothes. He'd claw at his pyjamas. He'd throw a tankard at Corporal Chates asleep in the opposite bed.

He did not like Wednesdays.

He hated them.

Loathed them.

Of course they didn't start badly; the soldiers' breakfasts on Wednesdays were good. On Wednesdays they had the Galley Cook and the Cacklesmith in Old Bridgeford. These two gentlemen spent the greater part of their week in New Bridgeford but they'd arrive after supper on the Tuesday to great fanfare, they'd stay long enough to make for the soldiers the one halfway decent meal they would get for the week, and then they'd be off back to New Bridgeford before Wednesday lunchtime. Corporal Beamish did not take breakfast on Wednesday mornings, he found his stomach could not bear the burden.

Because on Wednesdays, at fifteen minutes after eleven, he had to get in that rowboat with eight convicts and row out to that wretched hunk of God Shit in the middle of the bay. He had to board that unsturdy vessel, he had to bear the wind and spray, just to drop off to that Rum Doxy's crack, John Dunnock, his be-frigged provisions.

Every Wednesday, every week, he could not bear it, his body could not tolerate the task. He dreaded it. He had not been made used to boats at any point in his life, he was not familiar with the ocean, he did not trust convicts. He feared it. It was his Hell on Earth and this was in a land that was itself the show of Hell on Earth, a bloody and poisoned wound; the fetid, rancid sore where Hell had burnt itself high up and high and breached and bleached and scoured the surface of this planet. Here they struggled to make their lives surrounded by the signs of Satan's infamy, they huddled together and suckled on carcasses around his doorstep. That trip in the boat was to leap across the Devil's threshold and make harum scarum passage down his hall.

Beamish had to battle that wretched ocean, he had to fend off the sharks; he had to beat back the claws of Satan. He had begged to be relieved of the task, and he'd been whipped for his temerity.

Beamish sat with his fellow soldiers while they took their breakfast. He smelt their bacon; he watched them eat. He could have killed anyone at that moment. He then had to march down into the yard and stand in the sun for a half an hour and listen to that bugger-boy's fart Shanker blow on his whistle and shout people's names. He would have allowed Sergeant Shanker to perform his concert for as long as Shanker chose, he could have blown his shrill whistle for an hour, shouted for a second—each moment was precious that delayed his wretched boat trip—but Cum-Seepage Shanker always wound up his dreadful noise at eleven o'clock.

Then Beamish had to march over to the Quarter-Master's Tent. It was there he collected Dunnock's provisions—*Damn it, he was fetching a madman's groceries*—and it was there he had to salute three people, two of whom he didn't respect in the slightest and, on this particular Wednesday, the third he despised. The biscuits, the flask of vinegar, the salted lamb, the potatoes, he put in a crate. They were checked by the captain on duty—this Wednesday Captain Naskin—they were double-checked by the Governor, and then they were triple-checked by Partridge, the Second to the Quarter-Master. They were bound in rope by the Governor. Then Beamish had to deliver the crate down to the docks, command a rowing team, and take it out to John Dunnock, where he lived in deranged exile out on the rock in the middle of the bay.

Wednesday mornings brought Young Corporal Beamish very low indeed. This Wednesday morning he took special care to break, snap or impair every item he tossed in Dunnock's crate, except the salt biscuits he would be keeping for himself. They did their checking and their counting and their binding up with rope, and sure then Young Beamish saluted those three Dumb Gluttons farewell. He promptly saw himself out and he spat in the dust. He staggered before the sun a moment then gained his stance, he ambled down the dozen or so steep steps that had been cut into the clay in the Quarter-Master's front garden. Then he lazed his way down to the docks. Under his breath he cursed the Governor and he cursed the Captain and he especially cursed John Dunnock. He practised the filthy limerick he was composing to amuse Sergeant Banaghan, he kicked at a tuft of prickles, lent over to scoop up a handful of stones to flick at the gulls and galahs and parakeets and lorrikeets and kurrapuuks aside the path and then was most alarmed to discover he had company. Captain Naskin had been walking along, two pace aside, the entire time.

Beamish straightened up immediately, improved his posture, corrected his carriage. He regulated his step.

He didn't like Captain Naskin, he didn't like the fact that they were walking alongside each other, and yet he now found himself speeding his stride to keep pace. He snuck quick glances up at Captain Naskin and assessed his mien. Captain

Naskin kept his eyes ahead him, made no smile or frown, and Beamish looked back down. The silence became intolerable.

'Sir.' He said and Captain Naskin ignored him completely.

When they reached the makeshift docks he called eight men away from Harman's pack who were dragging a great tree from the former Customs House, and had them carry to the water's edge, the rowboat. Captain Naskin stood waiting.

'Well, I'll be off then to take Dunnock his provisions now, Sir, then.' He said. Captain Naskin spat forcibly into the ground angrily, and then ground it in with his boot. He stepped into the rowboat where he sat at the fore.

'Blow me if you won't be coming with us today, Captain Naskin?' Ventured Young Beamish.

Captain Naskin scowled at him, shifted his coat tails clear of his buttocks, and then stared vaguely away at the horizon.

The row out to John Dunnock Rock took about an hour; it was a rough trip, the water was choppy and the wind was always fierce. Often the rowers found themselves rowing with all their might just to keep themselves in place. This morning, whilst conditions were normal, Beamish found it particularly unpleasant. Captain Naskin was clearly not in a chatting mood, in fact he now spent his time chewing upon a stick he had with him, cleaning the thing of bark.

Beamish was not at all fond of Captain Naskin, he disliked the man's manner, he knew he had few scruples. There was not a soldier nor a soul in Old & New Bridgeford who thought well of Captain Naskin, they all avoided him like he bore the Malmsey or the Palmsey or the Plague or something like that. For the soldiers it was not an honour to be assigned to one of Captain Naskin's expeditions; it was a grave misfortune. This was not their habit or general course, do not get the wrong idea about these fellows, they were not by nature belligerent or lazy, in fact the soldiers leapt at the opportunity to pass their duties under Captain Bridewell's command, if it involved a five mile march they were happy to do it. When it took them out to the swamps where the mosquitoes were mighty fierce, when it saw them off to the North road where there was no shade to be had at all, or even back down to the gully where those trunks needed clearing, they would not give a grumble. If it was time spent with Captain Bridewell they knew it would be time fairly spent. That he would value their labours, he would share his rum, he would listen, join and match them in ribald conversation. Not Naskin. He was a stinking queynte. They could not bear to serve by him. If he were to announce that he was leading an expedition to Paradise he would scarce find a man to accompany him. If they were under the command of Captain Naskin they would break as much as they could, allow as many delays as the convicts could devise, demand as many rest breaks as was permissible. The man was nothing more than the bold syrup of a donkey's pleasure and if they could trouble the fellow's life they took delight in so doing.

Captain Naskin was despised by all, and that common dislike was feeding a hate of its own. Captain Naskin did not welcome the enmity of every person with whom he shared this earth; it tore him to pieces. He was occasionally unsure exactly how he had come to find himself in Hell, but that residence was made worse knowing that each other demon despised him. He hated the fact, the hate was a poison, it was a troubleful hate, a venom that so filled Naskin it could be seen in his eyes, it spilled out in the spit that came from his mouth, was there in the bark of his voice, in the tremor of his aspect. It simmered and it simmered and were it finally to boil it would prove a hate so mighty it would lay beyond government.

Beamish was not altogether happy the man was in his boat. They reached the rock.

It was a horrible rock; it was a hateful place. Understand that, and understand also that the whole land itself was horrible and hateful. The whole continent was made out of nettles and fire and poison. This rock was one of the worst bits. It showed not a speck of fair life upon it, not a weed, not a grasp of grass, not a plant or a flower, and certainly no form of shelter. The rock itself had nothing but death left in it, the wind was full of needles, and the sharks didn't even think the need to conceal themselves.

Were you to have somehow compelled this the home of your worst enemy, it would have been beyond you to sleep an untroubled night. Fortunately, John Dunock was nobody's worst enemy. He'd been shipped out here a week after they arrived, nobody in Old & New Bridgeford remembered why, and nobody gave a hoot. They all secretly quite liked the idea of having their mad old hermit out off on his island.

Except Young Beamish on Wednesday mornings.

'John Dunnock, I order you to make yourself seen.' He said standing up in the small boat that had been stilled about fifteen yards shy of John Dunnock Rock.

There was no answer from the rock, it remained as silent as before. The water around it made a little noise, the waves lapped its edges. There was a thick strap of seaweed that flap-flapped in the wind like a tear of bunting. It was caught on the branch of a great, grey sunbleached tree that had floated all this way out to the rock and had somehow become affixed.

Apart from the waves and the seaweed there was not a sound from the rock, and more importantly, there was not much more to see.

'John Dunnock, I order you to make yourself seen.'

The rock didn't make a move, though this time one noticed how high the barnacles grew up its sides—*were they a speck of fair life?*—how cold the wind was. A few of the rowers shifted restlessly. Captain Naskin moved forward in his seat. Young Beamish stood patiently.

'Where is he?' Whispered Captain Naskin urgently.

Beamish didn't respond. Perhaps he hadn't heard, perhaps the wind blew the question away, perhaps he had heard but didn't wish to reply, perhaps he didn't know the answer. Truth be told, he was trying to work out what a seagull far over there had in its beak.

'Where is he?' Hissed Captain Naskin, putting his hand on Beamish's shoulder and shaking it roughly.

'He's over there, Sir, behind that top bit of rock. See the bit up there that looks like the top hind leg of a horse? He's down there behind it.' Said Young Beamish and he pointed, not at the location on the actual rock but at the location on some imaginary and certainly smaller invisible rock he had somehow visualised before him. He pulled back the cuff of his sleeve and carefully reached over his invisible diorama and pointed to a bit over behind it.

His sleeve was the sleeve of a soldier in the New South Wales Armed Corp and hence it was bright red with a smart trim of royal blue that ran its length. The cuffs were white and the button was gold and sparkly.

One of the convict rowers saw Young Beamish's arm stretching over so strangely and thought it looked like a rainbow, a rainbow with clouds and a sun and all and a rainbow that arched over and pointed to a little mini-John Dunnock hiding behind the invisible mini-rock that Young Beamish had somehow magically created before his very eyes.

'Where on the actual rock?' Said Captain Naskin and to the rower's eyes the invisible mini-rock vanished immediately.

'Behind that top bit.' Said Young Beamish.

'Well, row around to the other side.'

'Oh no, Sir. Not there, Sir.' Said Young Beamish, and he was instantly strengthened in his unexpected resolve by the supportive grumble and huff of the rowers. He added, 'He hasn't yet thrown all his shit, Sir.'

Captain Naskin had not the slightest idea what that last sentence meant. He wondered if it would be a disgrace to confess so. He thought through it again and a second time could not see sense in the statement—*He hasn't yet thrown all his shit, Sir*. He wondered at the shame he would have to bear if he professed ignorance, and he weighed things up, and he figured he could pull it off.

'What are you saying, Beamish, you stinking drop-tray?'

'He has not thrown all his shit, Sir. He saves his shit, Sir, he hoards it up.'

Young Beamish had explained all this before, to anyone who would listen, and he had explained it a number of times. He didn't even try to hide the fact that he was annoyed to be re-telling it. It was common knowledge that John Dunnock throws his shit at passers-by. It disgusted him that Captain Naskin didn't know this detail of life in Old & New Bridgeford. He made no attempt to conceal that disgust.

'He'll soon lose patience and then he'll throw himself out. We can wait here. He can't throw this far. Then we'll drop off his provisions and then we can leave.'

'Rubbish. Row around to the other side.'

Young Corporal Beamish didn't like this unexpected turn of events, but as he had fully expected an unexpected turn of events from the moment Captain Naskin sat down in the boat he had spent the row out here becoming resigned to it. He tapped one of the rowers on the shoulder and pointed them all to round the rock via the top end with the dead tree sticking out of it.

The rowers groaned as they settled back on their hard and splintery seats, knowing that they had been directed to go the long way, the more arduous way, but knowing also that it was the way that minimised their chances of being hit in the head by John Dunnock's shit. They were grateful. John Dunnock was well appraised of this strategic manoeuvre and he took swift advantage of the tactical opportunity it allowed him. He was all action, darting and racing around that rock like a sprite. It was an offensive offensive, I am atickled to advise you, the shit was soon falling from the sky. John Dunnock only got off one good shot, it splattered on the bow and flicked up onto Captain Naskin's boot.

As they rounded the tree and the sweep that was the far side of the rock came into view, they were duly greeted by John Dunnock. His naked body was filthy and clearly not tended by a sane man. He was thin and bending over, his hair and beard ragged and matted, his putrid hands clasped tightly on his fetid buttocks, drawing them open to afford all people on the boat a clear view of his anus and of his fine crop of Dilberries. Though I personally deplore the pun, an untrammelled view of his arsenal.

'Shoot him.' Said the ever-reliable Captain Naskin.

'Is that Naskin?' Said John Dunnock, straightening immediately. 'Is that Naskin?' He asked again, clambering his thin body behind a rock. 'Why if I ever get my hands on you Naskin I'm going to wring your filthy neck, you stinking...'

'Shoot him.' Repeated Captain Naskin, not for a moment feeling any danger to his neck.

'John, we've got your food.' Said Beamish.

'...he's a thief and a cheat and I'd whore his mother to shame his name.'

'Shoot him at once.' Said the thieving, cheating son of a woman Captain Naskin, and Beamish said,

'John, make sensible yourself.'

And his words worked. John Dunnock stood bolt upright and with his hands above his head, he stepped out from behind the rock. Captain Naskin was the next to speak and he said,

'Lie down on the ground, flat like a dog. Like a dog, fool.' John did so immediately. Young Beamish directed the rowers to bring the boat up beside John Dunnock Rock, not at all sure where to drop off John's provisions on this side of the island, and finally settling on the flat bit that looked like an upturned butter dish.

At the moment when Beamish was confident he could heave the crate up and over the side and securely upon the rock, and was about to do so, the boat rocked violently, he lost his footing and his left arm fell down deep into the ice-cold and dangerous water, and he caught sight of Captain

Naskin standing and stepping from the boat onto the island. He said,

'Come on Beamish. Get that crate unloaded.' And he walked straight by John Dunnock and up to the top of the rock. He considered the view in every direction, and then wandered off to have a look at the tree. The rowers helped Young Beamish disembark, and then heaved the crate up beside him. He wandered over to stand with John Dunnock.

John Dunnock had turned his head sideways and was resting his cheek on the cold rock. There was nothing in his face or his eye to suggest madness thought Young Beamish, he looked like a normal man who was in a dangerous situation and who was working out the best way to survive it. His breathing was regular and did not for a moment suggest panic; however, Beamish noticed that the word *Gloucester* seemed to be escaping from his lips.

'You've scratched the word *Gloucester* onto your rock.' He said. He could see it; it had been scratched in.

'No I haven't. It's part of the rock.'

'No it's not, you've scratched the word *Gloucester*. I'm sorry John, but it's not worth my back to conceal it. Captain Naskin, Sir. He's written the word *Gloucester* on his rock.'

'He can write every bloody word he knows on this rock, he is never going to leave it. He's got five minutes to open that crate and remove his provisions or we'll be taking it back with us.'

'Go on then, John.' Said Young Beamish the Dobber, and when Dunnock had scampered from his place, his absence revealed that there was a small ring scratched in under the word *Gloucester*—it had been hidden by his thin shoulder—and that this ring had a line coming out of it. Beamish knelt down. The line curled up gently and bumped into a whole lot of other smaller rings and these rings had words near them too. *Cheltenham* and *Burford* and *Witney* and *Oxford*—the man had left out *Eynsham*—and the line sped up and the little rings grew more and more numerous until there was this almighty great ring, all subdivided and crossed with lines and a meandering thread, and written beside it was the word *London*. Lines traced out in all directions. With his finger Beamish followed one line that went out the other side of the mighty ring and he traced it as far as *Colchester*.

He followed another to *Luton*, and up past *Nottingham*, and on as far as *Leeds*, and stopped when he arrived at that point which was as far as John Dunnock had reached. He looked at the virgin rock, imagined how it would appear when John had sketched in his roads and rivers and hamlets and towns, he looked at the vast and choppy ocean that lay just beyond it, and said,

'You don't have room for Scotland.'

'I'll squeeze it in.'

John Dunnock was crouching by the crate. He had with him a large stone that had been chipped at and chipped at and ground away at until it resembled the basics of a rudimentary knife. He was using this thing to cut through the ropes that secured his crate. The crate had never had rope on it before, he was amightily concerned. Captain Naskin was pushing at the tree with his feet, trying to dislodge it, just killing time and seeing if he could.

Beamish took the short wall to *Thurso*, looked at the ocean beyond, and then looked back down to *London*, and wandered over to *Norwich*.

'You'd have been better off laying it out this way, John. If you had have put *London* here you would've had all this space stretching out for Scotland.'

'It wouldn't have been right.'

'...and look, Devon would have fitted perfectly in here, you should lay it out...'

'It wouldn't work, Sir. I am about removing this rope and cannot chat.'

'Devon should go here.'

Young Beamish pointed angrily at his feet.

Dunnock pointed angrily at the sun.

'The sun doesn't rise from Dundee, Sir. It comes up over St Davids.'

Beamish immediately saw Dunnock's point. His island was around the wrong way. He had England all around the right way in relation to the sun, he just didn't have room for it. Beamish crouched beside Dunnock. He was never going to get his way through those ropes in time. Beamish looked at Captain Naskin and wondered whether he had really meant his five-minute time limit. He released his knife from his belt, dropped it by Dunnock's feet and kept an eye on Captain Naskin. Dunnock didn't miss a beat, he magically swapped the knife for the ill-conceived implement and set swiftly and more effectively upon those ropes. Beamish looked at the great stretch of flat rock over Dunnock's shoulder and said,

'That's way too much space for Wales.'

'Well perhaps you and those rowers would like to each grab an end of my island and turn it around the right way.' Answered Dunnock as he broke the ropes. He then removed his meagre provisions, briskly concealed the remains of the rope behind his back and passed the empty crate back to Young Beamish, whilst he secured the crate's slide-slates beneath his foot. Beamish didn't like being made to sound foolish by a convict, particularly one who was said to be a madman.

'Captain Naskin, he's done, Sir. We can leave.'

Captain Naskin returned to Dunnock and Beamish. 'Not much of a place is it, Beamish? It's a place a rodent would live.' He said and then he ordered Dunnock to lick the faeces from his boot. He stepped into the boat.

Beamish claimed the box lid from Dunnock and passed it and the crate to one of the rowers. He had another quick look at Dunnock's England and then, steadying himself on one of the other rowers' shoulders, he suddenly remembered for a moment something he thought he'd seen, and he demanded from John Dunnock the remains of the rope. He awkwardly climbed aboard the dinghy and took his place. He directed the men to row them back to Old Bridgeford.

At no point did he retrieve his knife.

Part I

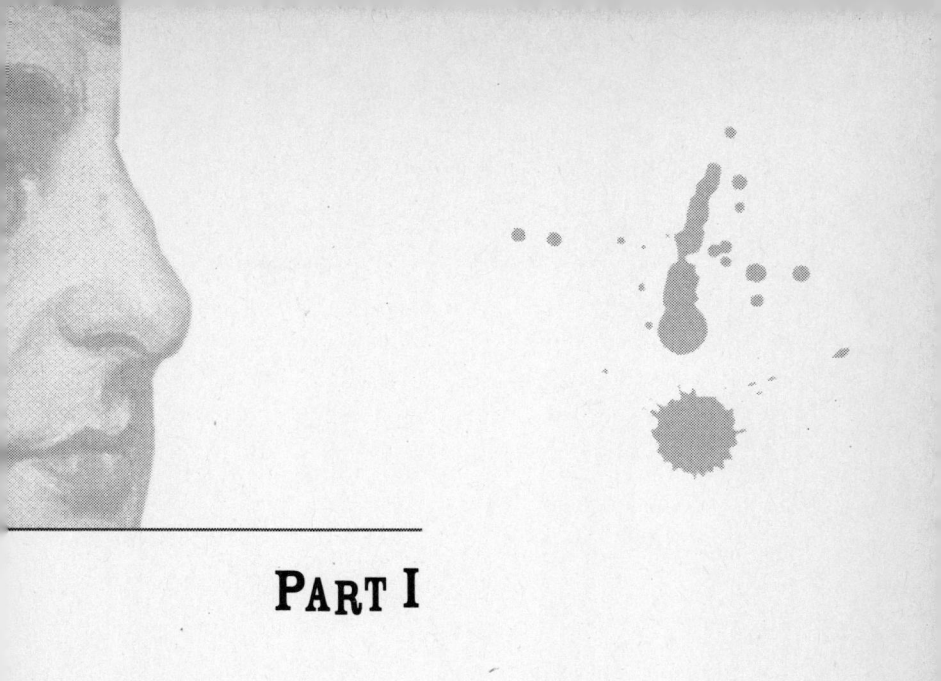

CHAPTER 1   DOCTOR WILMOT

Young Doctor Wilmot had worked admirably hard on the grounds and surrounds of his cottage. He had worked unflaggingly, he had requisitioned convicts to work unflaggingly on his behalf; he had dug and threshed and laboured and toiled until he got his land right, and it all looked terrible.

One of the first things the Governor had done when they had landed at Old Bridgeford was allocate generous packages of land to the officers and the trained men. He'd marked off squares and halved and quartered them, he had hammered in white stakes and he had secured guy ropes between; Governor Rantallion was securing the land. It was a sight to see those lines the next morning, the ample dew had clung to them, they sparkled like silver wire in the morning sun, gleaming like intricate scars in the low-lying mist; he had lain himself down a web. Doctor Wilmot's allotment was one of the best, it sloped down to the main thoroughfare, they set his cottage on an angle such that it caught the evening breeze, it swept back three hundred yards to the base of a fine craggy hillock that shared its shadow during the hottest parts of the day. Doctor Wilmot worked on that land like a Trojan.

He spread out great sheets of canvas and secured them down with rocks, he beat out the bushes, he dragged out the logs, he bludgeoned all the bracken and clubbered the ferns. When a week had passed he drew back the canvas and burnt every dry stick and twig and shred and seed and snarl of foliage. He hated the flora in this land; hated the lacquer on the leaves, hated the unholy knots and gnarls of the branches and roots; he thought the seeds and seed pods horrid, ungodly things; he loathed the rich and derisive colour of the flowers, they were hot and florid and sticky, poisonous, sweaty and fetid. They as scared him as a woman's pudendum.

When he finally had every piece of plant life banished from his domain, when he had staked out his plain of dust and clay, he spent all of his time sweeping it free of seeds and pods and berries, and when, having done so, he found there were still free hours in the day, he began clearing the yard of the Cartographer next door. When he was asked by the Cartographer to kindly desist, he started working his way up the cliff at the back. Doctor Wilmot was not going to stop until he had cleared this land of every plant on it. It was his priority, he held it should be the priority of every person in that colony. He believed they should have crews of convicts out there wiping every bit of life from that land, burning it, stomping it, killing it and then casting the whole lot out into the ocean. When he met with the officers and other gentlemen on Wednesday evenings at Jack Robinson's Cabin, he passionately argued the case. The other officers were either not interested or too busy, they either thought him mad or held that as the land's only doctor he should find himself other tasks to address. He had frequent disputes with the Colony Botanist. He would leave those Wednesday night suppers at Jack Robinson's Cabin disappointed and disheartened, he would lie back on his bed with his eyes wide open and stay there for hours, listening to the Jungle stealthily creeping back up on him.

Alone and mighty affeard of the forest, astutter and astammer and barely able to reckon an incident, Young Doctor Wilmot was a poor regal wreck about that small colony, his floundering constant, nervous and a twitter, he spent his time mumbling and cursing, beating back the Jungle from his land and yet, and yet, and yet there were still moments in a day. Ever the doctor, he knew there was much in his behaviour that bespoke madness and always the cold scientist he knew the best prescription for that condition was the company of one's fellows. In his still moments he would seek out their society, prevail upon the stilling hand of his fellows, visit the bakers and attend the rooters, wander by the docks and rile the fishermen, urge the bracken clearers to greater industry, by the banks of the billabong mark the washerwomen curse, sit silent and attentive upon Jack Robinson's Porch listening to Fat Old Jack and the Putty Eyed Native, a long forgotten drink warming in his hand, minding their unfaltering prattle. He soon learnt an idle and eavesdropping medic was not a fellow oft welcome in a colony of convicts and rogues, but

Fat Old Jack and Our Bennelong didn't seem to mind him being around so he spent most of his time there. Still and silent, a long forgotten drink warming in his hand, and listening to the tall tales and yarns of the two old rakes, listening to their words, listening to the murmur of their voices.

Jack Robinson requires some explaining. He did not resent the fact that his name would immediately click off in a hearer's ear an association—*(something occurs) . . . before you could say Jack Robinson*—it did not trouble him. I have a friend called Gordon Bennett who does not enjoy the association with a mythological counterpart, I know of a family of Brays who tire at people commenting upon the exploits of their namesake, my own name can be jumbled about and reordered to invite similar comment and I do not enjoy it.

It did not bother the Jack Robinson who found his home to be in Old & New Bridgeford because he was *the* Jack Robinson. In England he was famed as an insulting and impatient person. This was in a time when towns were villages and cities were towns and any person could be found interesting, they did not need to have been on the television— it did not exist. So poor were his manners that often he would visit his neighbours, declare himself to the butler and be so chapped by the time spent waiting his host's attendance in their hall, he would be gone before his name was announced. *(Jack Robinson has scarpered) . . . before you could say Jack Robinson.* He was in fact flattered that his name had entered the commonplace language as a saying to express a very short period of time, it was not a burden or a blight, though I suspect it was a considerable one for all of the other Jack Robinsons.

Perhaps he was relieved; his name could as easily have entered the language to describe a man who has murdered his older brother. Perhaps he would have seen some shame in that.

Chapter 2

'Twas said of Jack Robinson that he was born with a silver spoon in his mouth, aye this was true, but he could not help but be jealous of the golden one with which his brother supped.

He killed his brother to get the fortune. A simple matter; he hated his brother who returned the affection. He resented the fact that his brother would get every penny of their father's estate, the brother had made it clear that there would be no disputing the will and consequently no informal allowance would be made for any reasonable claim Jack Robinson might make. His father would not countenance debate upon the issue. Jack Robinson was a learned man, he was a clever man, he was shrewd and astute, he quickly devised a way of removing his brother from the equation. Damn her soul, his mother did naught about it. He knew of certain poisons and potions, and secreted them into his brother's food and drink at every opportunity.

CHAPTER 2A

'Twas said of Jack Robinson that he was born with a silver spoon in his mouth, aye it was said, 'There was too little of the wooden spoon about his apples.'

Unfortunately, the death of his brother commanded the attention of a number of other learned men and they quickly devised the way Jack Robinson had gone about removing his brother from the equation, they also knew of certain potions and poisons and precedents and prosecutors. Jack Robinson was astonished and surprised by the fervour with which they pursued their case. There was no one of note who had particularly liked his brother; he was in fact universally reviled.

CHAPTER 2B

'Twas said of Jack Robinson's brother that he was born with a silver spoon in his mouth, aye it was said, 'What a pity it had not been a silver steak knife.'

Jack Robinson was astonished and surprised and stupefied by the fervour with which they pursued their case. He needn't have been. England was founded on the passage of wealth from first-born male to first-born male. It was the modus operandi and raison d'être of the place. When he dared to take the life of a first-born son it was the mightiest crime conceivable, each Judge and Lord and General and Earl wanted him extinguished; he would have done better to commit regicide. This brotherhood of first-borns came down upon him with every weapon they had in their armoury and they blasted him across to the other side of the earth; he should have wondered that they had not killed him.

Governor Rantallion was not a simpleton, he was stern and he was cruel and he was hateful but he was a very capable thinker. Further, he was a second son himself; additionally, he knew Jack Robinson from college and enjoyed the man's company. He knew the nature of Jack Robinson's crime and he knew that in the colony of Old & New Bridgeford there was not any other older brother of Jack Robinson to tempt the man to greater infamy. He allowed him his liberty.

Jack Robinson was a better man in this land without his history: it freed him up. He was a fine host with an abounding appetite for grog, food, conversation and merriment and it was not long before the officers and captains, the Governor and that vain rabble of scientists and artist-types took to congregating at his house most evenings. Whenever possible in manner and fact, and certainly each Wednesday night.

Jack Robinson loved these Wednesday evenings he hosted considerably. He spent the three preceding days ensuring he had ample supply of rum, beef, pork and sausage, bread, beer and scotch, he spent the three succeeding days chuckling as he remembered this or that particular ruse, quip or jape, frowning as he further debated unresolved or unconcluded disputes. He would sing out to this or that fellow for clarification upon a half-forgotten argument, would pay a visit upon this man here to have him further explain that point there.

Jack Robinson lived a bright and merry life, a life of splendid indulgence, spurious indolence and pleasure, and this fact was known by every single soul of that colony; the overworked guards and lower soldiers who drank more of their own sweat than they did of scotch or rum, the labourers from the ships and the freedman serfs who heaved and carted rocks and stones all day and at night handled bread of similar taste and texture, the mass of convicts who knew the man to be one of their company and knew that three days had been well spent were they survived. The beleaguered Cartographer, the insane Doctor, the sea-wary Corporal, the heart-broke Young Corporal, the Spanish Convict sick and sundered, the bitter Captain, the debauched Old Priest and the mad, dear Astronomer, the Convict obsessed with seeing the hermit and the boat rowers and the rock hewers and the bracken clearers and the branch throwers, the convicts hauled for theft, debauchery, insurrection and murder, the pickpockets, curs and pimps, the Pure-Fetchers, the Bluey-Hunters and the Sawney-Hunters and the Dead Lurkers and the Snoozers, the Drag Sneaks and the Cat and Kitten Hunters all knew of Jolly Jack Robinson's splendid life of merry pleasure and sparse activity and they all knew that he was nothing more than a fucking lag.

They were breaking their knuckles and watching the skin fall from their bones and burying their fellows and he was living splendid with the gentry. Why, he was a gentry of his own. Now, that man had poisoned his brother. All their crime had been was stealing a cheese or cutting some illicit keys or pounding and then pounding a whore. Better that they had murdered a Lord?

Sure he was a friend of the Governor and a fine host and a cheery fellow but by the letter of the law his heart should have been pulled from his mouth. He should have been dragged through the town behind a cart and his stomach should have been filled with sticks and twigs and coal and his head should have been sundered by an axe. By now his bones should be swill for pigs. Here he was, living a life of splendour, free to days of idleness, days of leisure. There were rumblings.

His rights to such privileges? That was questioned. And was the Governor right to bestow such privileges to a common criminal? The question was asked. What of his ability to govern? What of his wit as an administrator? What of his competence? What if they knew about this at home? Many questions were asked.

The floorboards of this land were a constant adventure. They had been sundered from the trees, set down in line, nailed into place, but within five days of incarceration they had done everything within their power to alter that situation. They had shrunk, expanded or shrivelled up like twigs, stretched from their nails, recoiled from the glue, twisted away from their bindings, wrenched themselves away from the cross & cuts and heaved up from the stakes and done all that was within their boardly wit to return to the forest where they had much preferred their condition. One could not cross a room of this land without tripping or staggering or being sprung over Westwards or being splintered and scratched. The firmament on which Governor Rantallion walked was more treacherous still. Oh yes, there were rumblings. The Governor hastily haphazarded up a circuit breaker. After the flag-raising in the square on the Wednesday he announced that Jack Robinson was forthwith Officer of Duties and Tariffs, Master of Exports, Imports & Sundry Trade, and First Captain of The Customs House. The Convicts and Freedman and many Begrudgers soon noted that the small colony did not have nor find any trading partners, no surplus to sell nor capital to spend, a fallen tree through its Customs House. The rumblings grew and rocks were cast at the Governor's quarters on three succeeding evenings. Jack Robinson was frequently stoned. There were greater demands that his situation be called to account. Governor Rantallion saw disharmony and dissent suddenly spark, flare and take hold about him, he was distraught. He enjoyed this fat fellow, they had been friends, allies and co-conspirators at college and his God-given opportunity to cut the man a break filled his heart with joy. He earnestly consulted.

'I am at a loss, Captain Naskin. I consider Jack Robinson a good man and see no reason to prolong his ill fortune. He is a worthy man and shall soon discover the manner by which he can prove that worth.'

'Nay, he is a fat, red bastard who drinks too much and should be flogged seven nights and see if he cannot think a better way to pass his hours.'

Governor Rantallion fast sought a second opinion.

'Yes, I see your dilemma.' Said the Colony Astronomer. 'Of course his languid life of comfort and ease must rile these hard-working people who daily battle up their existence. Stick a firecracker up his generous arse and make him earn his keep.'

The Governor tossed up his options and considered his courses, the rumblings were a calamitous riot now. On Wednesday past seven convicts died of malnutrition; the same day had seen Fat Robinson consume half a tube of tuna paste. The man was a delight, a friend, a companion, a person to whom Arthur Rantallion had sworn eternal allegiance, a mate, a comrade, a fellow member of the Governor's own merry band of Sherwood, and Governor Rantallion realised that he was going to have to cut him off and cut him fast. Free him up and cast him away, let the wolves have their way, Jack Robinson was going down, disappearing fast, best be free of the fellow. 'Then let me be Prince Hal.' Thought Governor Rantallion.

Jack Robinson was a learned man, he was a clever man, he was shrewd and astute, he quickly devised the manner by which he was fast being removed from the equation and he fast conceived the manner by which calamity could be averted. Jack Robinson knew of certain precedents and precursors. If he must sing for his supper then he would sing a merry tune sure, but it would be his song, his.

Jack Robinson soon proposed that he should learn the languages of the natives. He had a good ear, a swift tongue, a gift for listening, a predisposition to conversation. By this manner he could learn what plants of this planet were fit to eat, which lands were safe, which black men honourable, which portents ominous. He bid that he should teach one of these black people English, and thus ensure fruitful discourse. He knew of one amongst the local natives he thought fitting for the project, a man of pickled eyes and awry limbs, a man of scratches, snarls and frequent curses, of like age to himself and a frequent visitor to their camp. A prickly fellow called '*Grr . . . Ich(k)idna*' whom the Englishmen had took to calling 'Our Bennelong'. Governor Rantallion saw such excellence in the proposal that on the following Wednesday morning at the colony assembly and flag-raising he so comprehensively praised the arrangement's qualities that the greater number of the soldiers and the fellows and the convicts reluctantly grumbled their approval, conceded that it appeared a vaguely meritorious suggestion, and agreed to give it a chance and reserve their judgement.

Jack Robinson launched himself upon the project with commendable endeavour and soon his gardens were alive and athunder with the never-ending tumult of their conversation. These two old roués soon nutted out a means of shared communication—half English, half Native, not so much a Creole but more a scatterfire pidginese, and they passed their days dining and drinking and arguing, riling and lampooning and conspiring freely.

'No, well that's where the trick is. The villain's wife recognises the handkerchief and the hero is well and truly appraised of his noteworthy faux pas. He has killed his fair and faithful wife, it's a dreadful situation, that's why it's so nifty.'

'All of these words, all of these things, they are about water. Kammen-kaah—see, he "free from water". Kammen-kaah see, it means he is "free from water". Dimmihaa-kaah—he "fly to water", follow him sure for he is "Mister Fly-to-water". See—it's all about kaah, it's all about water.'

'When he divorced Catherine of Aragon all of Europe recoiled in disgust, my homeland was the pariah of all the civilised world. But this was just a mischievous intimation, an impish portent of the unholy misbehaviour he was about to wrack.'

'Well, our fellow, he is not that much like him, but our big fellow, our like-your Henry, he is a snake. He's a big fellow, our Nammanook. He's a big fellow, he eats heartily like your fellow, your Henry, he's sleeping on the trees, he's sleeping in the sun.'

Alone and fearful of the Jungle, Young Doctor Wilmot spent much of his idle time visiting Jack Robinson, often silent and attentive on his porch, a long forgotten drink warming in his hand, and listening to the tall tales and yarns of the two old scoundrels, listening to their words, listening to the murmur of their voices, plucking at stray weeds in his environ. He would attend while they argued and they mumbled and mimicked the intonations of each other's speech. He would note it when they found the two words for the same object. Dr Wilmot preferred the native's word for the bend in a river but he preferred his and Jack Robinson's word for the bend in an arm. He thought it particular that both words for a crocodile were so similar and of a common type and yet wondered that the native's word for sand should bear so many syllables and have no sibilant character at all. Kammendali struck him as being a meritorious word and he repeated it to himself beyond earshot of Jack Robinson and the native. He liked the English word Chimera and the native word Bunyip but the word he liked most of all was the native's word kurrapuuk. Heard the word spoken by Our Bennelong and he liked it immediately. Kurrapuuk. It was a type of bird hereabouts that looked like an owl, with dark greasy feathers and big eyes and it waddled around the Jungle like an old woman struggling with luggage. Dr Wilmot liked the hint of a hiccup that hid in the word, he liked the look of the word, he liked the way it sounded. If his life afforded him the opportunity to write down the word he would. He'd be straight back to his diary and he'd write it down, first thing, on the top line.

Kurrapuuk.

Then he'd sit back and look at it, trace it with his finger, and then write something after it. Something like '*Day*' or '*-seen Day*' or '*seen today down by creek*'.

After about a month he learnt to *centre* it. I know this for a fact; I have assiduously studied his diaries.[1]

Kurrapuuk.

That way he could write before it '*Day I saw a*' or something like '*Today by creek I witnessed a*' but it was obvious it was the first thing he'd written, there it would be in big bold letters and in beautifully penned letters and with all these other scrappy little words around it.

---

[1] When reading these documents it's extraordinary to note how profoundly and quickly his obsession shifts; he clean forgets about his fear of the Jungle.

Kurrapuuk.

And so an obsession shifted. He would then go on to describe the circumstances that had led to him seeing the kurrapuuk.

Some days he wrote nothing else but page after page of the splendid word, written tenderly and with affection by a man who had a great regard for fine penmanship, and considerable skill at the art.

*Kurrapuuk Kurrapuuk Kurrapuuk Kurrapuuk Kurrapuuk
Kurrapuuk Kurrapuuk Kurrapuuk Kurrapuuk Kurrapuuk
Kurrapuuk Kurrapuuk Kurrapuuk Kurrapuuk Kurrapuuk
Kurrapuuk Kurrapuuk Kurrapuuk Kurrapuuk Kurrapuuk
Kurrapuuk Kurrapuuk Kurrapuuk Kurrapuuk Kurrapuuk
Kurrapuuk Kurrapuuk Kurrapuuk Kurrapuuk Kurrapuuk
Kurrapuuk Kurrapuuk Kurrapuuk Kurrapuuk Kurrapuuk
Kurrapuuk Kurrapuuk Kurrapuuk Kurrapuuk Kurrapuuk
Kurrapuuk Kurrapuuk Kurrapuuk Kurrapuuk Kurrapuuk
Kurrapuuk Kurrapuuk Kurrapuuk Kurrapuuk Kurrapuuk
Kurrapuuk Kurrapuuk Kurrapuuk Kurrapuuk Kurrapuuk
Kurrapuuk Kurrapuuk Kurrapuuk Kurrapuuk Kurrapuuk
Kurrapuuk Kurrapuuk Kurrapuuk Kurrapuuk Kurrapuuk
Kurrapuuk Kurrapuuk Kurrapuuk Kurrapuuk Kurrapuuk
Kurrapuuk Kurrapuuk Kurrapuuk Kurrapuuk Kurrapuuk
Kurrapuuk Kurrapuuk Kurrapuuk Kurrapuuk Kurrapuuk
Kurrapuuk Kurrapuuk Kurrapuuk Kurrapuuk Kurrapuuk
Kurrapuuk Kurrapuuk Kurrapuuk Kurrapuuk Kurrapuuk*

CARRION COLONY

Kurrapuuk Kurrapuuk Kurrapuuk Kurrapuuk Kurrapuuk
Kurrapuuk Kurrapuuk Kurrapuuk Kurrapuuk Kurrapuuk
Kurrapuuk Kurrapuuk Kurrapuuk Kurrapuuk Kurrapuuk
Kurrapuuk Kurrapuuk Kurrapuuk Kurrapuuk Kurrapuuk
Kurrapuuk Kurrapuuk Kurrapuuk Kurrapuuk Kurrapuuk
Kurrapuuk Kurrapuuk Kurrapuuk Kurrapuuk Kurrapuuk
Kurrapuuk Kurrapuuk Kurrapuuk Kurrapuuk Kurrapuuk
Kurrapuuk Kurrapuuk Kurrapuuk Kurrapuuk Kurrapuuk
Kurrapuuk Kurrapuuk Kurrapuuk Kurrapuuk Kurrapuuk
Kurrapuuk Kurrapuuk Kurrapuuk Kurrapuuk Kurrapuuk
Kurrapuuk Kurrapuuk Kurrapuuk Kurrapuuk Kurrapuuk
Kurrapuuk Kurrapuuk Kurrapuuk Kurrapuuk Kurrapuuk
Kurrapuuk Kurrapuuk Kurrapuuk Kurrapuuk Kurrapuuk
Kurrapuuk Kurrapuuk Kurrapuuk Kurrapuuk Kurrapuuk
Kurrapuuk Kurrapuuk Kurrapuuk Kurrapuuk Kurrapuuk
Kurrapuuk Kurrapuuk Kurrapuuk Kurrapuuk Kurrapuuk
Kurrapuuk Kurrapuuk Kurrapuuk Kurrapuk (sic.) *Kurrapuuk*
Kurrapuuk Kurrapuuk Kurrapuuk Kurrapuuk Kurrapuuk
Kurrapuuk Kurrapuuk Kurrapuuk Kurrapuuk Kurrapuuk
Kurrapuuk Kurrapuuk Kurrapuuk Kurrapuuk Kurrapuuk
Kurrapuuk Kurrapuuk Kurrapuuk Kurrapuuk   Kurrapuuk
Kurrapuuk Kurrapuuk Kurrapuuk Kurrapuuk Kurrapuuk
Kurrapuuk Kurrapuuk Kurrapuuk Kurrapuuk Kurrapuuk
Kurrapuuk Kurrapuuk Kurrapuuk Kurrapuuk Kurrapuuk
Kurrapuuk Kurrapuuk Kurrapuuk Kurrapuuk Kurrapuuk
Kurrapuuk Kurrapuuk Kurrapuuk Kurrapuuk Kurrapuuk
Kurrapuuk Kurrapuuk Kurrapuuk Kurrapuuk Kurrapuuk

*Kurrapuuk Kurrapuuk Kurrapuuk Kurrapuuk Kurrapuuk
Kurrapuuk Kurrapuuk Kurrapuuk Kurrapuuk Kurrapuuk
Kurrapuuk Kurrapuuk Kurrapuuk Kurrapuuk Kurrapuuk
Kurrapuuk Kurrapuuk Kurrapuuk Kurrapuuk Kurrapuuk
Kurrapuuk Kurrapuuk Kurrapuuk Kurrapuuk Kurrapuuk
Kurrapuuk Kurrapuuk Kurrapuuk Kurrapuuk Kurrapuuk
Kurrapuuk Kurrapuuk Kurrapuuk Kurrapuuk Kurrapuuk
Kurrapuuk Kurrapuuk Kurrapuuk Kurrapuuk Kurrapuuk
Kurrapuuk Kurrapuuk Kurrapuuk Kurrapuuk Kurrapuuk
Kurrapuuk Kurrapuuk Kurrapuuk Kurrapuuk Kurrapuuk
Kurrapuuk Kurrapuuk Kurrapuuk Kurrapuuk Kurrapuuk
Kurrapuuk Kurrapuuk Kurrapuuk Kurrapuuk Kurrapuuk
Kurrapuuk Kurrapuuk Kurrapuuk Kurrapuuk Kurrapuuk
Kurrapuuk Kurrapuuk Kurrapuuk Kurrapuuk Kurrapuuk
Kurrapuuk Kurrapuuk*

Page after page of it.

He devised a rather ingenious way of writing the word such that it could be read both upside down and rightside up.

When the normal affairs of his day did not afford him sufficient opportunity to observe kurrapuuks he sought them out. He studied their habits, he followed their runs, he learnt their patterns, he tracked them into the bush.

He saw what they ate, he found their nests, he nestled their chicks and he wrote it all down. He brought them as many of those terrifying black beetles as the convicts could catch and he would carry these out to the kurrapuuks in two tin pails held at arm's length. The kurrapuuks didn't care much about Dr Wilmot. They pecked at him for a while and charged him a couple of times and then they let him be. He worked out what was the berry substance with which they lined their nests and he wrote it all down.

He was a talented artist with a sure hand and a keen eye. He would study them for hours and he produced hundreds of fine sketches. In the forty or so paintings he made he captures their form and shape perfectly.

He wrote page after page describing their calls and their song, the sound they made when warning others or greeting others or calling others to a meal. They were excellent mimics, in his diary he writes:

March 9. Today I encountered two KURRAPUUKs in the small gully of fallen bark. They were watching a little magpie—a young male—stalk a brown beetle. He was a skittish fellow this magpie, it took him some time to secure the beetle's capture, he found an hour wanting for the task. He watched the little beetle with his smart head cocked to the left and then to the right. He strutted up to the beetle and he hopped straight back. He flew up on to a branch and then he flew straight back down. He flittered and he fussed. When he finally summoned the nerve to step forward and claim that brown beetle, one of the kurrapuuks sang out, he did so in a way that shot straight up to the branches and then bounced back down and filled the bush with its urgency. It was the call of a female magpie in trouble, specifically, this fellow's mate. Little

Magpie cocked his head up, took two steps backwards and then flew off immediately. The kurrapuuks then erupted in glorious and hearty song, their bodies shuddering and their feathers dishevelled. They sat down on the ground and composed themselves. Then they wandered up, crossed the grove, and one of them snapped up the beetle.

You can see all of this character in Dr Wilmot's paintings; he captures it in their eyes and in the taper of their beak, you can see that they're smiling not grotesquely, not like a bird with a human smile, but like a bird with a bird's smile.

Dr Wilmot's studies and sketches, his expansive and exhaustive notes remain the pre-eminent reference on these birds, they are used by historians and ornithologists to this very day.

As a gift to future generations it is a gift of considerable measure. What dismayed his contemporaries was his discovery that they couldn't eat them. That the kurrapuuks were not tasty. That and the fact that he was never around. He was always off with his frigging birds.

Chapter 3   The Colony Cartographer No. 01

The Colony Cartographer was at his wit's end.

He was not a skilled mapmaker, he was not a talented artist, he did not have a sure hand nor did he have a steady eye. He had an infected thumb and his eyeglasses had been smashed. His eraser was lost, his pencils were blunt, his ink was brackish and sepid and his pages were damp. He was in a land where every man was being stretched to the extreme of his potential, and he had been stretched way beyond the capability of his. He was being required to make maps, maps, maps and more maps and it was driving him mad, mad, mad.

The Governor would have an idea—*'Send out some convicts to drag the tree trunks from the North fields and send out the Cartographer to record the surrounding areas'*—and off the Cartographer would be sent.

'We are off to further the West Road. Bring the Cartographer to map its course.'

'Have a party of convicts drain the lower swamp and dispatch the Mapmaker to chart its former shores.'

'I require a relaxing ride. Bring me my mount and bring me the Cartographer, his skills will be of the essence.'

The Governor was oft having ideas like this. The four I have described above all occurred in the same afternoon.

The Cartographer was being rushed hither and thither, he must map this land here, and then he was raced willy-nilly to map this land there, and then he was rushed over there and yonder to map that land there. It was more than any one person could reasonably be expected to bear.

And not just to draw one map, to draw many maps. There was one for their use here and there, one for the Home Office in Britain, another for the Ministry of Trade and the Ministry of Colonies and a fifth for the Ministry for West Winds. Then one for the Portuguese and one for the Spaniards and one for the Germans and Dutch, and one for the Belgians and then one for the French.

These were fantastical maps these last ones. They could be fictions, they could feature mighty crags, and mighty canyons, they could be swamp-ridden and pox-ridden and filth-ridden and unrideable. They could be marred by great plains of salt or vast fields of ice, it didn't matter, their essential purpose was to dissuade any other Europeans from having an interest in this august Southern land.

Governor Rantallion (for that was the gentleman's name) made quite clear the purpose of these maps, he exalted the Cartographer to excel and spare no labour in their execution.

'*These maps are intended for the use of the enemy . . . or . . . suspect nations. We know spies who know spies who know operatives who will deliver these maps to those who need see them. We do not wish the interest of any Hogs or French or Dutchmen or Hounds. Draw a land that will perturb them. Do not interrupt . . . I want many maps from you. For the Spanish and Portuguese I would emphasise the marshy qualities of the land, draw it a bog, I have seen their homelands, they do not like it too wet underfoot. Be silent . . . For the French I would play up the tropical qualities, they have established a foothold in North Africa, they prosper in Quebec, they have mastered sand and snow, perhaps we should test them with Jungle. For the German maps draw deserts, they do not like it dry. I know nothing of the Belgians . . . I once met one who was afraid of heights . . . perhaps you should draw lots of mountain ranges. I'll leave the details to you, just draw me a whole lot of maps that shall alarm Europeans.'*

The Cartographer was then hurried from Governor Rantallion's company. He found himself alone on the porch of the house, he wondered that he had been so summarily dismissed and hung around long enough to confirm it as the case, he sat down for a while and then wandered off.

And after he commenced the journey to his own quarters, he would look West, he would look South. He would check North over to his left and then he'd turn around and defer his travel and have a good look East. He knew that to execute the commission he would little require the assistance of his imagination.

The whole place was a funk hole.

For years this unknown territory had been marked on the maps of Europeans with the phrase '𝕳𝖊𝖗𝖊 𝕿𝖍𝖊𝖗𝖊 𝕭𝖊 𝕯𝖗𝖆𝖌𝖔𝖓𝖘'.

The Cartographer saw little in the unholy spread of this land to refute that educated guess.

He held this opinion both figuratively and literally.

Figuratively he saw 'Dragons' here because the whole land reeked of the hand of Beelzebub. Each inch of this land was a vile mockery, the plants were debauched profanities, the natives were the spawn of evil, the wildlife were absurd and stunted mutations. This land was vile, it was evil and alive and rancid, it was the vomit of Satan, it was the tongue flick of dragons.

And he meant it literally. There were actually dragons here. *'Great reptiles that slowly lumbered out of the wild Jungle and breathed out the rancid fire of their breath and then made feast upon that person closest to them.'* He writes of them at least five times in his diaries: *'These dragons that were swift upon us and made bloody havoc of our company'*—to my mind, they must have been goannas—*'I saw a pretty place to make camp and ordered some men to clear the fallen branches when sure we were met with one who had made battle with St George.'* Yes, goannas who had perhaps fallen asleep in the scrub and been woken up, stumbled out to have a look and stink out the place, and then taken a chomp out of somebody's leg. They scared the Dickens out of the Cartographer, he was horror-struck by the creatures.

He drew lots of pictures of them in his maps.

'**Here There Actually Be Dragons**' he wrote in Big, Bold Letters.

This land terrified him, he was overwhelmed by the number of maps he had to draw of it, he was fearful for his beloved as she endured these last four dangerous days, he was scared of the lizards and he was pretty tired anyway because the land was awful hot. He thought himself a steadfast, stout fellow, a resolute man not at all given to complaining. He was frightfully mistaken. One could not meet the man without hearing in tireless detail of his woes and misfortunes. So he was delighted on that day when the Governor asked him to draw up plans for the women's quarters. Imagine his general despair—he is at this point a reasonably likeable fellow—he had just spent the morning being urged by the Governor to add poison-dart-blowing tribes to a nicely rendered mountain range. He had earnestly fought for the integrity of his chosen profession and capitulated immediately when the Governor threateningly mentioned some of the special quasi-gubernatorial powers of his own chosen profession. Then all of a sudden the same fellow says draw up some huts for the women. It was a splendid commission. Imagine his delight. Ponder for a moment his great joy and then as quickly, defer it.

The Governor was not delighted, he was slightly pissed off. When the Governor finally decided it was probably about time to build proper quarters for the women—after the stockade and the munitions store and the Governor's quarters had been built, after the temporary courthouse and the makeshift pier and the interim lighthouse and the Interregnum Blarneyhouse and the Captain's Cabin had been constructed, before the permanent lighthouse but after the garrison stables and at the same time as the men's quarters were established and set in place and risen by hand and gently stoked into being and were erect—the women's quarters were knocked up. The Governor begrudged the task at the time and then bid his bubelous mind to be free of the thought.

The Governor cared so little about the women that he certainly didn't care to enrage them. He had been happy to see them bed down these last months between and beneath the branches and the canvas and the canopies stretched from tree to post but their clamouring grumbles and the approaching rains had increased and encroached and so he sent down his Cartographer to build their quarters however they wanted. He didn't care, he didn't want to know. If it required four huts with sixteen beds and eight huts with four, six dormitories with thirteen and half a dozen of three and a provisions hut, it was fine, he had the supplies, he did not have the interest.

He had not the faintest idea why the women had been shipped out on this first expedition, they should have only arrived after a year or near twelve months from landing, by then he could have had the place built. But they were here now, so the Governor wanted them fenced off and shut away; they could perform a few menial tasks around the place, and then after five months and half a week he would fully introduce them.

He cared not to think about women at this time, he had objects to build.

The Cartographer was gleeful. He was made well aware of the generosity of his commission, he had ample and varied material at his disposal, he had the space to create. And he did so excitedly and with great imagination. He had watched these women, he had noted how they behaved, he had kept an eye upon their doings and when it came time for him to make a little village for them he did a terrific job. He sketched in a messy little cluster of one and two bedroom tents—a nasty little scatter of crude cabins that could have branches set across them to keep in the cool, with side flaps that could be raised to let through the low evening breeze. These messy little dwellings all seemed to share the same meeting place, there was a common area where the women could do their washing, a large eating area where they could meet and share with food preparation. He planned these humble homes for the fifty or so women he had seen sharing each other's food, plaiting each other's hair and removing each others bugs. He planned a grand big easy-to-build barn for the centre, a grand dormitory, it would immediately catch the eye of those wicked old molls and their fetchers, they would think it a castle. He would fill it with a warren of shadowy attics and dark spaces under stairs, sneaky cupboards and secret dens. Its floorboards would let through the chill. Its walls will draw the damp. The windows he shall place too high to share a view, too small to share the light. He planned a sweet little eight-sleeper for those quiet old dears who all shared a fondness for Cornwall. When he almost had his job done he allowed himself some time to daydream, to idly fantasise. On a new sheet of paper he started to vaguely sketch the moats and towers and turrets of the mighty fortress that he planned for down the back corner, the mighty drawbridge and the great unscaleable walls that he was required to build if he was to stand any chance of keeping the Spanish Girl alive.

Chapter 4   The Colony Cartographer No. 02

The Cartographer had watched these women, he had considered how they behaved, he had kept an eye upon their doings and, believe me, that scrutiny had been returned, though the female convicts could make little sense of what they noted. Little was understood about the Cartographer, all that needed to be understood was that he was out there. It was wondered why he bore the title when Dr Wilmot was so clearly more skilled at the task.

The Provost Marshall was sometimes amongst them but it was well understood that he was grieving a dearly loved wife left in England. Captain Naskin was known to them but he was sin, pure sin. They all knew old Jack Robinson came amongst them but somehow Geraldine Larkin had got her clever little hooks into him before anyone had seen. They knew Pitt the Judge Advocate but he was a vain and horrid person full of all the bile and distemper common amongst men lacking height, he had the face of a ferret, the manner of a ferret, the character of a ferret and he was said to have a member the size of a child's thumb. The Botanist sometimes was with them, he'd grub around amongst them and help dig in their weeds. As they cleared away the bracken he would point out how the syrup ran up the stem, how the pods were on both side of the leaf. While they heaved those logs out of those gullies, he would gently draw the thorns from their fingers, rub cool lotions on their scratches, distract them from their pain with frivolous tales whilst he sutured their ruptures. It was clear that he preferred the company of other men.

Little was understood about the Cartographer. He seemed to just sit around, drawing jagged little scratches in his books and on his charts, his steady hand twitching like he had bowel bugs, like he had the rickets. Some thought him sly, some thought him handsome, others had judged him a simpleton; he had never been seen to hit a person. He had not the vaguest thing to do with the women and for some reason he was out there. He was the most desired man in that Kingdom.

CHAPTER 5   THE COLONY CARTOGRAPHER NO. 03

The Colony Cartographer was not a simpleton. He knew that he could not build a fortress for the Spanish Girl out of mortar and stone. It had to be made out of words and air, artful layers of circumstance and cunning, a labyrinth of lies. The Spanish Girl could not be hidden away in a castle of rock, pine and keep, she must be smuggled away in a wraith of intrigue and craft.

'God knows, if I had my druthers,' thought the Colony Cartographer, 'I would pick her on Wednesday myself. But I don't want my own dear lady friend to whom I have taken a fancy, having her own face sliced off cruelly with a rock.' And unfortunately for the fate of the Spanish Girl, that opinion was shared by what seemed like all of the gentleman of Old & New Bridgeford. They had been here for almost six months and by this time each man of the colony was known of to every woman, every woman was known of to each man. They had all made their connections, contracts and enmities and it appeared to the eye of the Colony Cartographer that all the deals and bargains and contracts had been struck. When Governor Rantallion billeted the women on Wednesday all the lines had been drawn up and matched up. Jack Robinson had his lass Larkin, the Second to the Quarter-Master had lined up the Portsmouth Whore, he himself had his pickpocket Megsy. There was not a good man amongst them who had not allied himself with some good woman. The Governor and his tawny-haired Linda Thomas, Sergeant Salt and the Convict Girl Becky, the Grimy Purse Lil Fletcher and that Stench of Cum Jack Shanker, Young Corporal Robertson and the Spanish Girl, but Young Corporal Robertson was a tadpole. He did not have sufficient clout to command a female convict in his service, he would not command a billetage, the Spanish Girl would be passed up and passed over and passed in and left amongst the gutter sluts who would cut her up nasty. She would be flayed.

The Cartographer saw the dilemma. The Spanish Girl needed to be billeted with a man who had not yet made a union and yet could command the services of a convict girl. Perhaps then the friendship with Corporal Robertson could flourish, perhaps it could flounder, what was of matter now was getting the Spanish Girl out of the women's quarters and to the refuge of a gentleman's cabin. But there was no such man to be had. Alas that the Most Reverend Father Pittman had insisted that he should be allowed to use the six rent boys as altar boys, or the six altar boys as rent boys or whatever, such a pity he had declined a woman to attend his manse.

The Colony Cartographer looked up from his notebooks and down into the valley where the town bustled and blustered and blundered before him and he noticed Captain Naskin swearing loudly and raising his fists to a goat that stood tethered in a field. He wondered for a moment at the nature of their dispute and then returned to his thoughts, took a moment to remember them, recollect them, reorder them, and connect them to his surroundings, and then, to his surprise, a solution suggested itself.

'Good God, Captain Naskin.'

CHAPTER 6   THE COLONY CARTOGRAPHER NO. 04

Oh God, the Colony Cartographer.

Alas, the Colony Cartographer.

He was one-part beleaguered mapmaker, one-part beau of the Convict Girl Megsy, one-part dutiful town planner, one-part saviour of the Spanish Girl, one-part *Herpetophobe* and seventeen-parts pillock. He was a tedious twerp and a supercilious twat, a pumped-up vain little stench of a man with a sly and underhanded manner that hinted he was forever conspiring at deception or was a frequent self-polluter but, alas, I must take my heroes where I find them.

The Colony Cartographer bundled up his maps and charts and plans and collected Corporal Robertson from the company of that woman who was the cause of so much consternation and bid they repair to Jack Robinson's quarters. They compelled the Colony Dentist from his oil cloth surgery and were joined by the Provost Marshall and then those four gentlemen converged upon the quarters of Jack Robinson, who had been napping when they arrived but he roused himself quickly and promptly offered them tea.

The Colony Cartographer fast brought his ideas to the conversation.

'Gentlemen, I have had a wonderful thought. Yes, and with one sugar.' He announced, interrupting the Colony Dentist's and the Provost Marshall's debate about the quality of the Provost Marshall's boots. 'We have all at some time bespoke a concern for the fate and fortunes of the fair Spanish Girl. I believe I have our solution.'

So... it was the heroic Colony Cartographer who first thought the idea that Captain Naskin might prove the key to the Spanish Girl's survival, it was *he* who first introduced the stratagem to the conversation of those men who concerned themselves with her preservation, it was *he* who most passionately argued the merits of the plan and volunteered its excellence, it was *he* who ultimately convinced his fellows of the idea's worth. Much to his surprise, and much to his concern, and much to his chagrin, it was *he* who was elected to expedite its execution.

In the manner of any person who unexpectedly finds themselves the mother of a rather sharp idea, he enthusiastically expounded upon its qualities until he found himself ensnared by its failings.

Its great quality was that it all made terrific sense and the plan should immediately be brought to the attention of Captain Naskin.

Its great failing was as above.

The Cartographer slunk about the door of Captain Naskin's Cabin and ruefully waited for the return of that place's occupant. He made a show of restlessly idling away the time and resenting this imposed idleness, but he dearly cherished the moments that elapsed before that fellow's return, he hoped they'd prove abundant and he prayed for Captain Naskin's eternal absence.

'Oh shit.' He said and then he reflected, 'Can't we all tell him this?'

He settled himself down upon the doorstep for a spell and then stood up and kicked at the burs that were staking a stronghold amidst the gravel of Captain Naskin's path. He nicked off down the back and checked out where the cliff burst upwards from the earth and he noticed the mine. He was as fearful of his quarry as any person has been in the history of hunting. He settled himself upon the rail and rested his eyes and almost fell backwards. He leant against the porch post and considered his folly and considered his fate and wondered at how he had found himself in this situation, waiting to proposition a resolutely horrible man with an offer beyond the comprehension of humanity. He shook his head and he looked around vainfully for someone to relieve him of that duty. He stood up urgently, and scratched the back of his head madly like he had a skull to wrench from its domain. His hands then debated each other like eagle's talons, he beat his brow and then rested exhaustedly against the porch rail and nearly fell over backwards when that tornado of restless energy that was Captain Naskin burst by him.

'I'll thank you to get your filthy fucking boots off my fucking porch.' Said Captain Naskin and he spat at the Colony Cartographer who rejoindered,

'I do not know that they are filthy.'

'Well then just you get yourself off my fucking porch.' Said Captain Naskin and he closed his door behind him.

'But...' Thought the Colony Cartographer and he corrected his collar, he picked a burr from his cuff and he straightened his vest hem, he shined his buttons as was his habit and he coughed and cleared the phlegm from his gullet and from his cheek and he knocked upon the Captain's door. Captain Naskin opened it a bare three inches and said,

'Don't you take a fucking hint, Pal?'

'I would ask, Sir.' Said the Colony Cartographer, straightening his shoulders and focussing his thoughts and rallying every bit of himself he had, 'Have you not checked your postbox?'

'What?'

'Do you not check your mail, Sir?'

'I have not thought the need.'

'Do you not then ever think the need?'

'Fuck off.'

'Sir I know for certain that you have received a letter.'

'It cannot be.' Said Captain Naskin and he grabbed the other fellow by the shoulder and forced the Colony Cartographer backwards till he was dangling helplessly above the steps.

'Sure there are only two people in this world who would try to contact me.' Said Captain Naskin, 'One is in England and does not have access to our rudimentary postal system, the other I had thought I'd left for dead in a burning cabin in Oregon. It terrifies me to know of his survival, it astonishes me to learn he has traced me to here of all the furthest reaches of mankind.'

'But it was I who got in touch with you.'

'I beg you pardon.'

'It was me who put a note in your postbox. It was I who wished to arrange an interview. For today. For an hour ago.'

'Oh, I see.' Said Captain Naskin and he paused and he rubbed the harsh bristles that grew like thorns from his chin, and then he smiled when he realised that again he could assume his nemesis dead. He released the Cartographer and said,

'Go on.'

'I wish you to be a whoreman to the Spanish Girl.'

Naskin stared and blinked in bewilderment, he had for a moment allowed his mind to wander and was again sitting in a pleasant green field watching a smart log cabin burning to the ground. This last statement of the Cartographer's had raced Naskin away from the meadows of Oregon and dropped him here some place in New South Wales in the midst of a conversation that he couldn't quite get a handle on.

He was for a moment bewildered and when he again caught the Cartographer's eyes those two men fixed each others glance and Naskin stared the Cartographer down below the floorboards.

'To be her Cumswab, to be a Whoreman to the Spanish Girl, to be her Wadswipe.' The Cartographer entreated.

'There can only be one sense in which your last statement bears inspection.' Said Captain Naskin. 'And its nature evades me. Come inside, Pal.'

'It is all worked out.' Said the Cartographer, chatting away and following Naskin into that gentleman's cabin and noting its general character. 'She is informally betrothed to Young Robertson—I do not know the details of the contract, it is a makeshift convict and soldier thing—I fear Robertson has not the slightest chance to command her commission on

Wednesday next. He had hoped to command the Governor's generosity, it was a fly-blown hope.* I think however we can convince the Governor to allow you a housemate. She will perform wifely duties by you Sir, she will tidy your home, she

---

* It was a fly-borne hope. Young Robertson had hoped that he might be able to command the Governor's affection on the basis of the fact that he had, in the last six months, saved the gentleman from certain death on three occasions. To Robertson's mind that equalled kudos. That by way of repayment or reward or agreement between two gentlemen he might be able to select a female convict to his service despite his lowly commission. And, yes, the Governor being the type of fellow he was, would have been quite ready to meet such terms. Unfortunately the Governor had never in his life heard of a person called Young Jack Robertson. He had a friend called Jack Robinson sure 'tis true, but of this other fellow he knew not a wisp. He didn't know that he was the fellow who had saved his life on those three occasions. To the Governor it had all involved just some interchangeable and anonymous lifesaving fellow dressed in red and white and gold. He hadn't really noted their names or ranks or anything, just merely thanked his lucky stars that there was one of them around. He had a crystal clear and frozen in time memory of their backs. He remembered the time he saw the back in front of him take a spear, and he remembered the time there was a great back in front of him the time that log swung round and would have taken his head off otherwise. He would never forget the back that so conveniently appeared the moment Moll Furnham tried to stab his dear vulnerable beating heart. He didn't remember their faces. Didn't know what the names of these terrific men with the lifesaving backs were. It never occurred to him that all of these backs might have belonged to the one person. He couldn't have cared less if truth be told, he had taken to thinking of these fellows as numbers anyway. He was referring to them as 'no. 54 over here' or 'thou thieving no. 109 over there'. He was going to make the practice law as of next Wednesday. He'd had enough of the lot of them.

will tend its garden. She will perform a whore's duty to Young Robertson.'

'My dear Sir, at this point it is only gentlemanly of me to slit your throat.' Said Captain Naskin and he begun unclasping his knife from his ankle when he suddenly decided he'd rather use the more gentlemanly looking knife he had sitting on a cushion of velvet in a finely crafted wooden box set upon his desk.

The Cartographer knew that Captain Naskin was not a man to mince his words, he knew the fellow would have no reservations about mincing some other person's neck. The Cartographer did not wish it to be his own.

'It is a matter of life or death.' He offered, desperately wishing to change the mood of the conversation.

'And this here shall soon be a matter of death or severe injury unless you fast depart.'

'She will die.'

'Then you'll be her companion, Pal, if you don't...'

The Cartographer saw that he just could not change the conversation, he was jumbling up balls but he was unable to change its course that promised such ill for him. Each word cut through the Cartographer like a pane of glass, he feared forlornly for his life, he saw his years of hope and aspiration amount to naught more than a sorry death here in this poor cabin, he stared death in the eye and he saw a dagger dance threateningly before him. It was the dagger Captain Naskin had just drawn from the handsome-looking box he had sitting on his crook-shanked and gumwood desk.

'You cannot slay me for this, Sir.' Said the Cartographer, finally finding the combination of words that would save his life. 'It *is* an ignoble task I ask of you sure; it is a grand and honourable one.'

'I beg your pardon.'

'She will die.'

'Who, Sir?'

'The Spanish Girl.'

'Who?'

'The Spanish Girl. The one I would have you tend.'

'In my anger, Sir, I had completely lost track of her. Extrapolate.'

'If you take her from the woman's compound you can save her life. She loves Robertson, he returns the affection, we can spare her.'

'How shall she die?'

'She will not be picked on Wednesday. You know the Governor has allowed that certain women can be selected to attend to the quarters of certain men of the colony. We have worked out who will be selected, the Spanish Girl shall not be in their company. We believe we can get you a pick Captain Naskin. I am pleading with you to pick her.'

'You misunderstand my enquiry Sir, let me rephrase it, in what manner shall she die?'

'When all of those other villains and molls twig that there might soon be another Wednesday when some of them may be picked, they'll make sure she's not picked then either. They'll cut her face off and they'll cut the face off every other pretty girl there. They'll scar these girls wicked. Then all that'll be left to the other fellows is a whole lot of wicked old bitches with the clappers. It happened in Adelaide, it'll happen here.'

'What do you mean, it happened in Adelaide?'

'Have you not been to Adelaide, Sir?'

'I have been there.'

'Have you not noted the poor quality of its people's appearance?'

'I have noted it, and often shook in horror.'

'Have you not wondered the cause?'

'I have wondered it a thousand and one nights.'

'There's your answer. They were born of the most hideous couplings the human mind can conceive of. These bizarre and ungodly unions caused horror in the heavens and compelled the angels weep. Each child of Adelaide is born of the horrendous and fetid ruttings of the most foul women and the basest men that this poor earth has had shame its surface. We think the Spanish Girl's worth saving. We want to get her out in the first stream. This is the only way we could think of doing it. Robertson loves her, Sir, he's pinning his life on this. We think she's worth it. She will be flayed, Sir, she will be grievously injured.'

'Then remind me, Sir, who is this woman?'

'I beg your pardon.'

'Who is this Spanish Girl, whose worth is so holy and so high?'

'She is the most beautiful woman in this kingdom, Sir. I cannot believe that you do not know of her. You play a bluff, Captain Naskin, and respectfully, I call it as such.'

'Take it how you like, what's the thing with Robertson?'

'He dearly wills this, he thinks of nothing else, he yearns for her.'

'Her?'

'She thinks well of him, she dotes upon him.'

'Dotes? I do not understand doting.'

'I'm not quite sure myself, but I think it involves furiously unpicking needlework, but see respectfully, Sir, this is not really about that, it's about somehow avoiding her having her face cut off with rocks and knives. This is the best way we could come up with.'

The Cartographer gazed beseechingly at Captain Naskin and put his hand to the other man's shoulder. His gesture was intended to heighten the noble and imploring quality of his speech but so shocked was he by the strength and furious heat he discerned beneath the Captain's sleeve, he could do nothing but immediately take his hand away and in its swift retreat his arm knocked a tankard from the table. Said Captain Naskin,

'Still, I do not think I have the need of a housekeeper no matter how many tankards you spill.'

'Again, Sir, that is not the matter. I care nothing for your domestic arrangements, they are your own to attend to in the manner you see fit though I would suggest there is about your quarters an overwhelming smell of foot. My issue is that of saving a poor person from a poorer fate.'

CHAPTER 7

This was the Wednesday after that.

There came a certain Wednesday when the Cartographer opened up his sketch book and laughed nostalgically at his fanciful stratagems of that day a week prior, smiled embarrassed at the towers and turrets and the great unscaleable walls, could admire for a moment the well-rendered cornicles upon the gate house and then dismissively scratch a big cross through it. There came a Wednesday morning when the Cartographer could turn his eye to the village of Old & New Bridgeford slowly growing before him and artfully sketch upon his pad the details of one small hut and before it draw an ogreous man in a military uniform and a very pretty woman in a very silly bonnet.

He captioned his sketch 'A *Captain of the Infantry and his housekeeper (PoHM)*'.

Because in three days hence, that would be the happy circumstance.

Chapter 8   Young Corporal Robertson

Young Corporal Robertson loved Wednesday mornings, he could barely stand to await them, he counted down their arrival, he mourned their passing. They made his whole week liveable.

He did not, on Tuesdays, do a thing that could possibly bring him any joy or pleasure or abandon, because that same panacea, that same balm or elixir or intoxicant, would fuck with his guts the very next day and he wanted to be sparky on a Wednesday, sharp and disciplined, sprighty and alive. Because on Wednesday mornings, at fifteen minutes after ten, he had to surrender his post by the provisional cabbage patch to the attention of Corporal Bierce, and escort the iddly-piddly Cartographer down to the women's area where the iddly-piddly Cartographer oversaw construction of the women's village. Every Wednesday, every week, they were nuggets of joy placed at seven-day intervals throughout his present life and without them he would have grieved, despaired, floundered and abjectly sunk into despondency. They were his moments of sunshine, these times he spent with the she-lags—particularly the time spent with the Spanish Girl—and they were thoroughly enjoyed by the women folk also.

The genial relationship between the convict women and Young Robertson had commenced from the moment they all boarded the great ship and the women noticed how decidedly comely he was and had developed and evolved during those times when he was set to march them on the decks, oversee their eating, guard them whilst they were abed.

He was astonishingly shy, not at all given to conversation—handsome though, damned handsome—short in his replies, frugal in his addresses, sparse in his commands, though he was frequently prone to thinking aloud. A melancholy still would oft be broke by Young Robertson suddenly announcing something, something like '*. . . and that's precisely what should have been done*', or '*. . . as far as I'm concerned behind the coal box was always the best place for it*', or '*. . . it should always have been red*', and then he would return, with embarrassment, to silence. These outbursts were always the capping off of a debate, the firm resolution of a silent discussion, the final attestation on an issue Young Corporal Robertson had internally been considering for some time and their profundity so impressive that they would unwittingly compel his voice. He was never forthcoming when asked what had come before, he would refuse each inquiry, not reply to any 'why?'. He would shuffle around, blushing and blinking, embarrassed and evasive, and any '*What were you thinking, Son?*' or '*What were you chattering about?*' was met with his crimson blushes, his stuttering and stammering and the timorous shaking of his head.

Well as we all know, women are crafty shrews and delinquent women are the craftiest. The female convicts soon devised the means by which the comely terrapin Robertson could be coaxed from his shell. They'd greet his sudden pronouncements with something like, '*Nay, that's the last thing you should have done, you stupid git.'* They'd say, *'Behind the coal box? What were you thinking fool,'* or *'Red as well as green, both colours stupid and ill-considered.'* Young Corporal Robertson's wit was not the equal of his considerable beauty, nor was it able to match such Machiavellian tactics and he would fast inquire, *'Really? What should I have done?'* or *'Do you truthfully think so?'* or *'Is that the case? Why?'* and from that point it wasn't impossible to get Corporal Robertson chattering, to get him to open up, to get him nattering on, to show them who he was. Young Corporal Robertson was a fine and respectable fellow.

His voice was pleasant, his timing accomplished, his storytelling skills honed and at times charmingly animated, though perhaps—it must be said—his limited vocabulary constrained the tales to one's dissatisfaction. He told these convict women tales about his people. He winked at the Spanish Girl and started spinning his yarns about the village where he had lived, about the well behind the church, the barn at the bottom of the gully, the old abandoned windmill and the monks retreat on the mountain peak. He told them tales about the twin brother of the Baker, about the mad mother of the Apothecary, about the new Schoolmistress and the day the owl roosted above her blackboard, about the poison in the Magistrate's wine, about the sheets of slate that rained from the Lens Grinder's roof, tales about the secret son of the Choir Master, about the fallen and sinful sister of the Charnel Smith's Dominatrix. Stories about his people.

After about two months aboard that convict ship, the Spanish Girl noticed that the little soldier's stories seemed not to make sense. That Mr Perkins the Cobbler had died when the trench caved it, he could not have been there three weeks later when the mule was shot. That the Seamstress had two brothers who were soldiers, neither was a Silk Boiler who could have visited her in July. That it was this neighbour here who had the four goats, not this other one there. When the Hornet Grinder turned up to three remote affairs on the very same night, and a week after he'd left for America, the Spanish Girl laughed out loud, and got kicked in the shin for her outburst.

Young Corporal Robertson danced those villagers through a hundred impossible loops and the Spanish Girl was pleased that she was the only one who had noticed. That the stories were really meant for her.

His voice was different when he told stories about his family, it had a deeper tone, it was more solemn, it sounded like a washed brass bell. It was certainly quieter. The stories were different too. They were still pretty stories but they weren't as colourful as the antics of the villagers, these stories were happy/sad. His mother must now be a tired old soul, his older brother had done her proud and it was a sorrow he had died so young, and his father was a weasel who had left her while she was still bearing this boy before them. She had kind friends. It was lovely to hear the way this boy had taken his brother's name before that of his lowform father; it lifted the heart the way that boy Robert had been a Da to this boy, brought him up to the best of his reckoning and been a constant support to their Ma. It brought tears to the eye to hear of how the barrel had fallen from the cart upon his head and killed him flat, killed the older brother of Young Robertson. He told them about how those boys went hunting frogs, hung from branches and from loft beams, made up the dinner for Mum.

These stories cheered a lot of those convict women up. They kept a lot of them sane.

They loved that family; they liked this boy. When he talked about his family he encouraged them to speak of their own, and when they did he asked them questions. And when everyone started up talking and asking questions it was almost what you'd call *a nice time* down there in the rank bowels of that rotten ship.

The amiable relationship between Young Robertson and the women prisoners continued when they landed in Old & New Bridgeford and whilst he saw less of them, and they less of he, they all enjoyed it when the other was around. He asked them questions about their health and welfare and listened when they told him more things about their family. He answered questions about his own. He was the best soldier to have guard them; all the others just bashed and fucked them.

Young Robertson sat down in what had become something of a central square in the women's area, the earth had been beaten flat and this area had become a place of common meeting purely by virtue of the fact that a lot of trudging was being done there. They trudged this way to the waterhole and they were trudged this way to the chalk quarry and they were trudged that way to the gate and these lines intersected at the point that had consequently become the meeting place. Robertson sat in the centre and rested his rifle across his strong sturdy thighs, these two mighty tree trunks that this man called legs, and that pressed hotly and like beaten bronze against his weather-starched and sun-bleached pearly cotton tights. He rubbed his rough fingers across his dry and cracked lips and whistled twice. It was a long drawn-out whistle, a lovely strong curve that just edged along steadily for about four heart beats and then finished with a sparky pip-pip. These two last notes were funny echoes of the first, the one higher, the other just a wee bit lower, each revealing a different aspect of the first. They giggled at the first note, they giggled at themselves. He was whistling a secret code. He repeated it.

The moment the Spanish Girl heard it she closed her eyes.

The Spanish Girl was applicant to her task; perhaps threshing sheets in a tub of soapy water or plucking bugs from that day's meat, perhaps forcing a union of stale water and wretched flour, drawing nails from a board. It is enough that you understand that she was dutifully about the task she had been set upon.

A few of the other women prisoners squatting and picking through straw and lice-ridden bedding, messing about her feet in a dank murk of lizard's leg and howlet's wing heard the whistle and they winked at each other and elbowed each other's ribs, they laughed their harrowing lecherous laughs and their cheeks clambered so high up their face they could do nothing but close their eyes. They slapped their hands merrily upon the ground and they urged the Spanish Girl to go promptly to her beau.

It should also be understood that these were the six or eight absolutely idiotic women, they laughed at everything, they smeared themselves with their own faeces. All that remained was to discover whether they were sheer mad women or merely complete lunatics.

Of course, the Spanish Girl was embarrassed by their ribald amusement.

She was completely embarrassed by her boyfriend, that he saw this ridiculous need to announce his presence with the ludicrous whistle. Everyone knew he was here, he was sitting in the broad daylight in the middle of the square. Everyone knew she would soon join him.

All the more sensible women prisoners looked at her with serious and varied glances that ranged between violent contempt and a more gentle pity, there were scowls and spits from the cutthroats and villains and petty tyrants, there was a vague glow of warm support that showed on the faces of the kinder women.

The Spanish Girl relaxed into herself and shook her head, she cleaved herself from the fear and reproach and doubt that idled ever-present in her character, she wandered forward to talk again with Corporal Robertson, who was kind despite his embarrassing whistle charade, who was well-intentioned despite his pitiable innocence, who treated her gently, tended her kindly and Good God let's be honest, in this wretched place, that was the only thing that was keeping her alive. It was feathering this unholy inferno with a soft glow of light. It was keeping her alive. He would treat her kindly.

As she went to sit with him, as she went to gently pamper the key that would unlock her cell, she was urged supportively forward by one of the mad and horrid bitches, the woman left a great palm slap of shit on the back of the Spanish Girl's dress. The Spanish Girl wondered if Young Robertson would detect the stench; she wondered how she would explain it.

But oh gentle mercy that she be free to consider such idle wonderments but, woe, the Spanish Girl was soon to be violated again, the Spanish Girl was about to be set upon again by one of the mad wretches, but this time the crazy fucking bitch had her a rock.

CHAPTER 9   DOCTOR WILMOT'S CABIN

Everyone of them who was racing to Doctor Wilmot's Cabin— Young Robertson racing before, and ushering convicts and carts from their passage, the Spanish Girl occasionally stumbling but running with strength, and the two soldiers beside her offering her support when it was required, speeding her pace when they got to the downhill bits, and the Cartographer running with all his strength and occasionally waving at them, three hundred yards before him, knew that there was absolutely no point in them doing so. That they were running to an empty house. That this house they were madly converging upon had been vacant for the eight hours preceding these events and would be vacant for the eight that would follow.

When they arrived at the Doctor's Cabin they spent a period of time affirming their intuition accurate. They stomped about his quarters, they called his name. They knocked imperatively upon the door to his privy, surveyed his barren grounds and searched the scrub that neighboured his fences. They checked under a big pile of canvas staked out, out back. There is no thing on earth as particular as a man set about a task he knows is pointless, I have noticed that such a fellow's industry cannot be matched. He can pursue his task with no limit to his zeal knowing that the endeavour is futile and, consequently, aware that there is no shame in failure. They raced wickedly about the Doctor's premises, those Soldiers Potter, Wilcox and Robertson, they called up to the branches of the highest tree, they spared no bush or pile.

They were almost set upon drawing his floorboards awry in pursuit of the absent surgeon when the Spanish Girl, ailed by her injury and distraught by their distemper, bid them be still. She allowed that there was commendable merit in their endeavours and thanked them for their industry but requested that they wait for Doctor Wilmot in a manner that should not manifestly increase her distress. She petitioned that they should rest a while and for her sake, patiently await the Doctor's return. This was wise on her part, part wise and part foolish.

Wise because there was no point to their stomping and clomping and raucous calling—the Doctor was off tending his birds—and foolish because—unbeknownst to herself—she was swiftly dying. I am no more a trained practitioner of medicine than I am a scholar of Nineteenth Century Australia. I cannot with any surety describe the precise nature of the Spanish Girl's injury. I do not need be. It suffices that you understand that the rock that had been thrust into her face had caused a grave injury, she was bleeding, she was bleeding swiftly, she was bleeding freely and swiftly and profusely. The woman who had struck the Spanish Girl was not a trained assassin—she was a fool with a rock. Concurrently, I am not a trained at nothing—I am a fool with a pen. Between the two of us we have contrived to place the Spanish Girl upon the threshold of death's door. Time is of the essence. There is blood everywhere. It is a peculiar conspiracy, the most bizarre concord of intent in which I have been a party, a strange and bewildering alliance that has spanned some one hundred and eighty years, this woman and I have colluded and conspired to render this great injury upon our prey, tore her face asunder and left her on oblivion's doormat and having rung the bell, secured our giggling selves in the bushes to observe her fate. It was the fool with the shit on her face and the cloth and pegs she tended like a baby who wrought the great damage, it was I who ensured that there was no doctor to tend that injury.

I really need to dissociate myself from this woman.

Having romped and clomped and called and hailed, the soldiers readily acceded to the Spanish Girl's entreaty, there was no fault in the manner by which they had sought the Doctor, there was honour in their application. And so they all found the best manner by which they could await his return. Wilcox drew a pack of cards from his pocket and, by the manner in which he revealed them, invited Potter to share a game of chance. Potter readily complied and Robertson made the journey from window to door to victim without relent. But woe the Spanish Girl. She spent the time becoming a rainbow. There were parts of her as pale as a badger's tooth, great blue and bloody bruises welling upon her face, great gluts of blood streaming down her cheeks and staining her neck and collar. On the one side she grew paler and paler still, but on the other she became more and more bloody, her side became redder and more sanguine, there was discord in her aspect, there was death in her condition.

They settled in Doctor Wilmot's first room and found the manner by which they could best await the Doctor's return, all but one. And they all fast understood that they didn't have time to wait until he got back from those birds. They had been waiting at the Doctor's house for about the entire amount of time it would have taken you to read all that intrusive stuff and the Spanish Girl had not stopped bleeding. The Spanish Girl was embarrassed by the amount of blood she was yielding, she earnestly tried to staunch that unending flow, the soldiers earnestly sought to assist her. All parties failed. She was bleeding profusely and to the eyes of the soldiers and the lately arrived Cartographer she was bleeding over-profusely.

They did not have time for Doctor Birdrutter to return from the bush, she was going to die. There was nothing else for it, they were going to have to call upon Governor Rantallion and hope for the best.

Chapter 10   The 'Gov'

Governor Rantallion had had two years training as a physician, he had for many years neglected the art but he hadn't forgot it. If he chose, he could with great skill apply his hand, and he had stitched up Thornton's gash on the thigh, he had somehow got that stake from Kennedy's shoulder. He could as readily rest it. He had rested it that night when Wayland found his leg beneath a log. Wayland had been slow to move from the path of Governor Rantallion three days prior, the Governor was equally tardy when repairing the other man's leg. He wasn't as quick to consider the wound, he paid greater attention to the sufficiency of the lighting. When he finally did inspect Wayland's leg he did so only long enough to register the considerable seriousness of the wound. He then readdressed the lights and called for a seventh lantern and wondered at the cleanliness of the towelling. When he finally did address the violent disorder of Wayland's leg, he unfortunately stumbled and rendered the injury greater. He stayed around long enough to pronounce the man dead.

Milton died when Rantallion bid him drink the wrong potion, Garfield died when Rantallion neglected the great rupture to his belly to restitch the gash over his left eye.

What Governor Rantallion had been doing was quite inexplicable. The soldiers couldn't quite find the word for what was going on, they all agreed *'sure, 'tis mighty strange'* but at the same time they knew it was all a hell of a lot stranger than just being mighty strange. (It was their era's want of the word 'nutso' that left their tongues ill-footed.)

He had let Young Ryder die and all the soldiers could really attribute it to was that the fellow was dumb-simple and foolish.

They looked at the Spanish Girl, they looked at the blood she was spilling and they knew they'd have to take the gamble. They had to race to the Governor's lodge and compel him, they had to pray that he found her meritorious, because otherwise she would die.

Chapter 11   Eek!! Captain Naskin

The soldiers were mightily concerned and so should they be. They all thought they were caught between a rock and a hard place. They were wrong, of course, they were at that time caught between a rock and an *even harder place still*, a fact that Young Robertson soon discovered. If I have been at all unsuccessful in conveying these fellow's reservations about locating Governor Rantallion in the time of the Spanish Girl's distress will you at least allow that I have, with some success, created the situation and circumstances where, to their understanding, unearthing Captain Naskin on this occasion would prove a grave disappointment.

It was Young Robertson who sped from the Doctor's Cabin to the Governor's quarters. He demanded the task and his affirmed interest in the matter disavowed any challenge. He raced with the greatest speed he could muster, showed such haste that he would rival the finest athlete. But he was not fast enough to dispel the danger to the Spanish Girl, not fast enough to assure her well being, not fast enough to allow you for a moment to be confident of her good survival. No, not yet. Young Robertson bounded up the path to the Governor's porch, and rent open the door—desperate and fearing for his beloved's life—he cast the frail door inward, allowing the dazzling light to dispel the brooding gloom within. He then returned the door to its hinges and hurried down the long hall. He espied Captain Naskin off to the left sitting in some other room somewhere to his right but so intent was he upon discovering the Governor that he dispelled the slight distraction and propelled himself forward to the Governor's study. It was empty, damned empty. If the vague impression of Captain Naskin sitting off to the left in some room was not sufficient to suggest the Governor's absence, Naskin's words did plenty to confirm it.

'If you're after the Governor, he's not here. It's just me here.'

And then there was silence for a few moments until Captain Naskin added,

'Me and Pissfart.'

Young Robertson returned to that vague room off to the left and discovered it to be a library. Therein Captain Naskin was reading a book, a book about how if you ploughed your fields in a Westward direction, the furrows would hold morning dew that might make all the difference in a harsh and dry Southern land. This was not the only book in the room, all the others lay well thumbed and discarded by his chair.

'He bid me be here at eight o'clock this morning that I be painted by this piece of frippery. I did not see him then and I have not seen him since.'

The piece of frippery was the Colony Portraitist who was standing by his great canvas and he nodded at Young Robertson by way of acknowledgement. It was a nod of greeting but somehow it was more than just a nod of greeting.

It was a meaningful and resonant and literary nod, artful enough to indicate that contemptuous insult was now a common occurrence in his relationship with Captain Naskin and need not be commented upon. Its art was in how manneredly it silently expressed this welter of information, it did so surely and steadily and it was not until the forehead rose to reveal the ironically arched eyebrow that one fully understood that one was not to speak of or note the cruel manner in which Naskin addressed his companion. Bandying around terms like '*pissfart*' and '*frippery*' like they were '*Gentleman*' or '*Sir*'. It was way too subtle for Young Robertson's speedy tongue.

'Sir, I think you speak of this man poorly. I demand that you apologise.' Said Young Robertson and the Colony Portraitist urgently clicked his fingers at the soldier and having commanded his attention he shook his head imperatively and with his hands seemed to press away the creases in an imaginary bed sheet. Young Robertson said,

'You idle, Sir. I demand at once that you beg your remission.' And the Colony Portraitist shrugged his shoulders resignedly and turned to re-address his brushes.

'That speaks well of you.' Said Captain Naskin and the Colony Portraitist did the equivalent of what is still referred to at the time of publication as '*pricking up one's ears*' (though the expression clearly wants for something) and Captain Naskin continued.

'There is no dishonour in standing to the defence of another fellow's. It is a chivalrous action and speaks well of your parent's tutelage. It's just that you are awfully ill-informed. This fellow and I have just spent the last four days in each other's company. We have discussed a thousand matters and thus discovered we disagree on a thousand more. We have tacitly agreed that there is no honour in the fellow worth defending. He is frippery and he is a pissfart. What do you want?' Asked Captain Naskin and he stood up and strode so purposefully towards the doorway where the young soldier was standing that Robertson could do nothing but surrender it. Captain Naskin gripped the frame in his hands and threatened to rip it from the wall so mighty was his grasp. He seemed to be ascertaining the direction of West.

Captain Naskin was having his final session with the Colony Portraitist. To the understanding of the Colony Portraitist this was not the final session at all, this was the fifth session, the seventh session would be the final session. Captain Naskin had decided there was not going to be a seventh session, nor a sixth for that matter.

The Colony Portraitist was the Botanist, we have met the fellow. He was very skilled at drawing the line of a new plant's leaf or seedpod, he could ink in its colours, he could mix paint to match its flower, he had spent two years studying art, when the Governor asked him to paint his portrait, he felt a warm shivery thrill. He was excited.

He took to the task with relish and he mustered every source he had at his disposal, his training, his good eye, his natural skill.* He painted a wonderful painting of Governor Rantallion, one can see the confusion and disorder of the man—it's there in his eyes, they are a hair's breadth from weeping, they are a welter of confusion; it's there in his stance, he is barely holding his body together. The Botanist gives you a feel for the strange sunlight of the place and in the background he does a fairly good job of a kangaroo.

After a while and after the unveiling the Cartographer wandered over to the Botanist's quarters and suggested that the fellow might like to test his hand a second time and the Botanist found himself in the difficult and enviable position of trying to negotiate a fair and proper fee whilst suppressing his schoolgirlish giggles. He was having fun.

Old Jack Robinson wandered over having decided he'd give it a go and the Botanist paints up wonders with his hearty corpulence, he is a man who has lived a dreadful life and he's had a wonderful time doing it. There is a particularly nice rendering of a kurrapuuk in the background. There is nothing but blank horror in the eyes of the Colony's Cornmaster.

---

* The paintings this fellow produced during those six months in Old & New Bridgeford tell one as much about the painter as they tell us about the subject. In his paintings the Botanist showed the good eye of a Viking, the steady hand of a Grecian, the good wit of an Indian and he clearly carried himself with sturdy and resolute Mayan knees.

He hides behind an emu. They're marvellous paintings, they tell you volumes about these spooked-out men cowering in this hideous landscape. Their petty deceits are all on display, their dreary vanities, their frail self-delusion; it can be seen in the tight anxiety of their pose—these are tight, tight men; it can be seen in their eyes—these are buckets of sadness.*

---

* I'm aware that at some point and at some time in the vast and renowned, long and glorious or obscure and ill-noted history of this novel there will eventually be the reader/receiver who wonders how on earth all these paintings somehow mysteriously survive the apocalyptic events that rendered Old & New Bridgeford a barren wasteland. Wondered about that bizarre unleashing of God's merciless fury, the insane inferno that annihilated all but a handful of those that were at home in that small colony, that brought great madness and treachery to the land, and yet somehow, miraculously, spared the paintings. Initially I stoppered this loophole at its logical point within the chronological structure of this manuscript, however the expansive nature of the information at that point did little to serve the tone of the novel, in fact it significantly disrupted it.

 I bring the following information forward, confident that the small hints to this story's outcome do not damage the novel in the considerable manner by which it was impaired when this pesky passage lay in it's logical location. In setting this passage here I both appease the pedants who would be unable to sleep happy without this extraneous information and concurrently straighten out a nasty kink in the road that was coming later on. It is a win-win situation. You will appreciate my foresight.

 '... *when the Botanist saw the great flames come trooping down the hill, when he noticed the convicts enacting their evil and bringing perverse vengeance even closer to his stockade, as he watched his compatriots die by his side and when he noted the departure of Naskin and considered the death of Rantallion and wondered for the safety of the Spanish Girl and rued not joining the expedition*

Captain Naskin thought they were shithouse.

He couldn't quite put his finger on why the paintings were fucked, but sure they were fucked. It would be pointless for Captain Naskin and I to now list our arguments for and against these paintings, I would recommend you go with Captain Naskin, he had the advantage over myself in actually having seen the gentlemen in question. Captain Naskin had looked at these paintings and he had looked at the actual fellows walking about him, when asked his opinion he would bark

---

with Young Robertson that had departed four days previous, he fretted. What was going on here was havoc. The fire was burning the flesh off him, the convicts were death in his eye. Good God, he had just seen the Cartographer shot. What had become of the Colony Astronomer? He would have liked to have been out on the boat with Doctor Wilmot going to John Dunnock Rock. Not here. Here he was going to die. When the Botanist/Colony Portraitist stared death in the eye he mourned the years lost and then devised how not to leave them nothing. He fetched himself away and gathered up every painting he'd made and he safetied them away to the shore. He kept them from the fire and he defended them till he was dead.'

When the Portuguese arrived a couple of weeks later one of the first things they retrieved from the wasteland of wreckage and rubble was the remarkably well-preserved paintings. They took these paintings and any stray gold coins they could find back to their caravels and they washed off the blood. They shipped them back to Portugal. These paintings and coins are still in Portugal and I spent the greater proportion of my Australia Council grant getting over there to have a look at them. It is a national disgrace that these paintings are not at rest in the land where the men who are depicted lived and died, made their stories and then bequeathed their names to that young nation's history. These magnificent paintings should be over here and in a special Museum in Canberra. I've said my piece.

some indecipherable sharpness and march angrily away. Later, he would return to again consider the painting. He didn't quite know what was wrong with them but he knew there was something. When he wandered over and watched the Botanist do his painting of Captain Bridewell he saw what was wrong with them and it all happened on the fifth day. He watched the painting of Pitt the Judge Advocate develop and the same thing happened. On day five it all went belly up. Same with the painting of Forsythe that was commissioned to mark him becoming the first and only man hanged in this Colony.

By the fourth day these paintings were wonderful items indeed. By mid afternoon on the fifth day they were perfect. On the first day they were grubby sketches, a multitude of different variations and unexplored possibilities and fruitless discards until a pose was found. On the second day they found a unity that was being mapped out on the canvas with bold strokes of charcoal and great furrows of black and red. The mighty swing of a shoulder was being etched in, a strong leg was being struck into the canvas. On the third day the colour was hurled into the painting, there were great torrents—nay, an inferno—in a man's forehead, there were great gullies in his brow. On the fourth day these different pieces of colour and force all joined and seethed into each other, the explosion of arm and the detail of hand joined with the sketch of the shoulder, and the neck came together with the head. All the different bits of energy were sewn together. On the fifth day, all through the morning, the Botanist/Colony Portraitist nailed in the detail, he put the small glints and the secrets into the eye, he put in the wrinkles and the tremors around the lips, then he stood back from the canvas and would pause for some time. Then he swapped his brushes. He unwrapped from a small white piece of cloth a slender long paintbrush with a point like a needle and a narrow shaft of onyx, and a small stubby little brush with soft fluffy bristles. He cooed at the brushes and they seemed to coo back to him. He stood back from the painting and looked at it a while and cocked his head. He then sighed and cocked his head the other way. He looked ruefully at his sitter who sat wondering what on earth could have compelled this turn of events, he looked back at his painting and sighed again, and then he began applying the make up. Why the fellow became a popinjay. He would be better suited to the court of a princess than this land I tell you. He was applying blusher to the cheeks, he was dusting down the sheen on the forehead, he was using his oils as mascara to bring out the allure in the eyes, the varnish was lip gloss. He was a strutting vain faggot, his subject would end up painted like a courtesan. Captain Naskin was not going to let that happen to him. He was reluctant to have his portrait painted—the Governor had ordered he so abide and unwillingly he so complied—he however would not consent nor comply with being decked out like a Shy Doxy's Caller.

Captain Naskin was having his final session with the Colony Portraitist. It was the fifth day, in the mid-afternoon, and Captain Naskin was about to ensure there was no further work done on the painting. The Botanist had just pulled from his paintbox a carefully folded piece of white cloth. Captain Naskin had a foolproof story and a knife. The Botanist revealed two new brushes. Captain Naskin unclipped his aforementioned knife and said,

'If you're after the Governor he's not here.'

He returned his knife to its sheath behind his left shoulder and then there was silence for a few moments until Captain Naskin added,

'It's just me here. Me and Pissfart.'

CHAPTER 12   CAPTAIN NASKIN

'One wonders at the duties of a Governor.' Continued Captain Naskin. 'It must have been a mighty task that has held his attention these four long hours.'

'Yes.' Mumbled Young Robertson, having not been able to stake a sound claim upon the area surrounding the doorway and yet at the same time feeling very comfortable about standing over here by the curtains and clutching on to the side cabinet.

'Come out of the gloom, boy. I'm sure there's ample space to await him outside.'

Somehow, Young Robertson found himself being scurried towards the doorway. He was delighted to let it happen, he was eager to escape. He was skipping gaily down the stairs and out through the Governor's fenceless gate when Captain Naskin brought him coldly and cruelly back to reality.

'What's the matter?'

'I beg your pardon?'

'What is the matter that brings you fast-eager to the door of Governor Rantallion?'

'Oh that. Good God, I'd forgot. It is the Spanish Girl.'

'I beg your pardon.'

'It is the Spanish Girl. She falters. She needs the earnest attention of a doctor and there is not a doctor to be had.'

'How is she ill?'

'Rock into the face—cheekside.'

'Deep cut?'

'Deep enough to have her bleed like the Jesus.'

'Bring her here.'

'Last I saw her, she has surely elapsed.'

'Show me to her.'

'You could as well show yourself, Sir, she's at Doctor Wilmot's.'

Yes, there was great haste in the manner by which Young Robertson took himself from the Doctor's Cabin to the Governor's quarters. It was nothing compared to the pace with which Captain Naskin compelled the return journey. There is at this point little in Captain Naskin to commend him to any reader who has persisted this far, everything about him should strike you as ill, however, I do entreat you to allow that he showed character when he learnt of the Spanish Girl's injury. So purposeful was the pace he set, so unsustainable was that effort, that it was not long before Captain Naskin and Young Robertson found themselves exhausted and had to make pause, gasping and fatigued, leaning over and resting their palms on their knees, heaving dryly and spitting the dust from their mouths, trying to find a tree to lean their backs against.

'It is a horrible place to take a blow, soldier, horrible. The cheek.' Said Captain Naskin drawing and searching wildly for his breath. 'I myself have taken wounds about the face many times. It can disfigure one for life, or, when tended by a fair surgeon, can be healed and repaired till it is nigh invisible. See this scar here?' Said Captain Naskin and he pointed to the left side of his face. The cheek Captain Naskin pointed to showed not a mark. On his other cheek he had a hideous scar, a hateful rupture that ran from above his eye, cruelly tore his cheek asunder, and disappeared under his unshaven jaw. But where Captain Naskin pointed and Robertson leant right in close to get a good view, there was not a mark, not a blemish.

''Twas surely a wondrous surgery for I see not a line of it.'

Captain Naskin stared at Robertson like he was an inexplicable idiot, he blinked, and then he stared at Robertson in a way that made the fellow feel like he was little more than a looking glass and then he blinked again.

'Sorry... I got the wrong cheek.' He said. 'See this scar here?' He said, and he pointed to his scar.

'Yes.' Said Young Robertson.

'Was both the patient and the surgeon.'

'I see.' Said Young Corporal Robertson and he and Captain Naskin resumed their journey to Doctor Wilmot's house at whichever speed Captain Naskin selected which in this instance was a steady and regular trot uphill. They were silent until that point when Young Robertson got his thoughts together.

'Excuse me, Captain Naskin. But, whilst you may have repaired your wound you certainly did a very noticeable job of it. Surely you should be the very last person of this colony we would think to have tend the Spanish Girl's cheek.'

Captain Naskin did not reply immediately, he did not do so for some time and when he did his reply bore only a thin veneer of civility. He had deliberately applied a thin veneer, he wished to make it quite clear to this insect that he now received his contempt.

'I worked with nails, nails and thread from a hessian sack. A river for a mirror. I was dying in the Jungle, you impertinent stench.'

'I respect your achievement. I just wonder whether this girl, in these circumstances, might fare a surer hand.'

'Listen boy, I can not adjudge what unholy butchery I will unleash upon this poor girl's head until I see the wound. I might then choose to resign the task to another person.

You seemed to suggest she was dying. That's why we ran here.'

Captain Naskin burst into Doctor Wilmot's hut disturbing Corporals Wilcox and Potter from their card game and scaring the living daylights out of the Cartographer who had sat so diligently by the window before the warm gaze of the afternoon sun and, as one would expect from a fellow of his type, had dozed off.

'She'll be dead in fourteen minutes. You should have done something.' Said Captain Naskin having checked the patient and then set about busily in different corners of the room. 'You were going to let her die because you fucking cowards are too scared to thread a needle?' He was picking up bottles and gathering up strange tools and grabbing a couple of one couldn't quite see whats. 'What would your mothers think of you?' He then settled down beside the Spaniard and, miraculously, he had the hands of a doctor.

'Well, she's not moving around much you've made sure of that.' He said as he pushed back his sleeves and then set his fingertips upon her cheeks and at that moment all the sound in the world disappeared and each fellow in that room looked at that very same spot of it. 'That'll make this considerably easier.' He said and he poked a thick needle into her skin and pushed it out the other side.

Young Robertson leant forward and found the entire affair absolutely gross. When that needle pierced her cheek it may as well have pierced his heart, his whole being felt that stab, it shot through his body like a slowly tumbling briquette, it surged back up like a sliver of hot ice that somehow beached itself around the base of his neck, it made his shoulders feel ticklish. Gross, he found the affair, gross but fascinating. He leant further still.

They all found different ways of describing how Naskin worked that needle. They did not hesitate to search their vast reserves of analogy and metaphor and slander and praise, to find the most extreme words to describe what they witnessed that day in the Doctor's room, where the beautiful and fair Spanish Girl lay defenceless to the rough and coarse hand of that hound's seepage, Naskin. Potter said it danced, the needle was a dancer, Wilcox thought it spun like a pin, a pin spinning on a lake of ice. Young Robertson thought Naskin stitched like a magnificent seamstress, like the King of all Seamstresses, but Young Robertson didn't know the half of it.

A seamstress works with cloth (he's such a knucklehead). Cloth is a two-dimensional conflux of thread being forced to share a relationship with another piece of cloth, and being rendered together with a sturdy piece of twine, what Naskin was working with was flesh. He had half freckles to match up with their counterparts. He had thin threads of membrane and tissue to piece together on an inordinate number of levels. He had skin to bring to skin, flesh to bring to flesh, he had to use stitching that should be seen to disappear as swiftly as it was applied. And just to the side was her dear strong nose, her still lips and above her peaceful eyes, below her listless tongue resting dumbly in her mouth, down further still her tiredly and anxiously beating heart, it was beating worriedly, desperately now, waiting for something it didn't know about to be set right, he had an awful flow of blood to staunch, and all about him these four bastards.

'Fuck off, the lot of you.' He commanded.

And after they'd left he muttered to himself,

'Jesus. They think this is easy?'

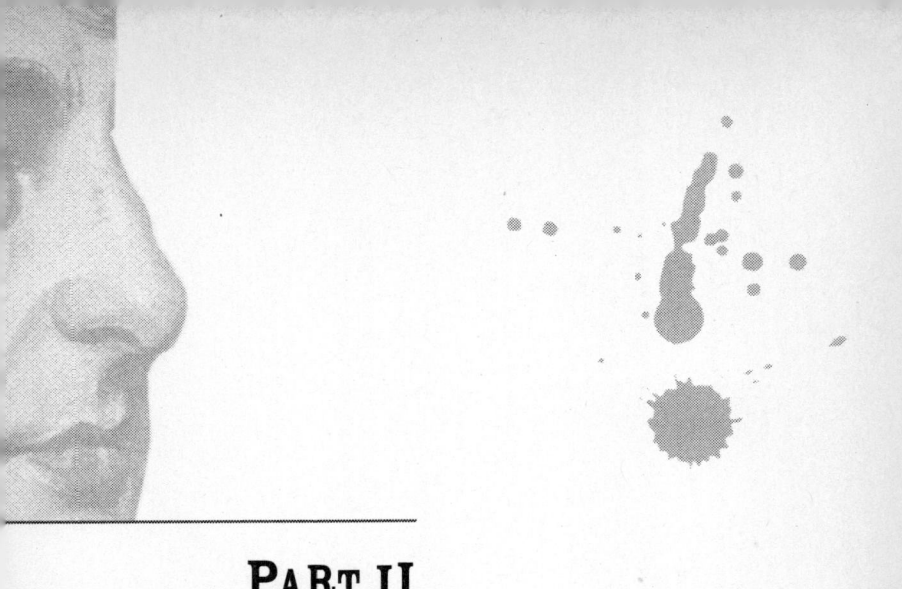

Part II

Chapter 13   The Colony Astronomer

The Colony Astronomer constantly had problems with the measurement incrementals of this world. He either frequently found that there were never enough or he regularly learnt that there were way too many. This was happening constantly and frequently and regularly. For example, the Colony Astronomer had discovered there were at least three other measurement incrementals by which one could describe the concept of 'often'. He held that that was not nearly enough. Further, to his theory, he did not hold that three dimensions were sufficient to describe the ways that things could be seen, he thought that there were about fourteen different degrees of *three dimensional* alone, there was the three dimensional you see on a foggy antipodean morning, there was the three dimensional you see when suddenly the stars aren't light specks and bright specks on a plane of black velvet but, rather, are vast lunar bodies set against the infinite realms of oblivion, there was the sharp three dimensional clarity you noted when a fork sat swaying in the neck of a bottle of red wine, the stray cork floating in the half-empty bottle and occasionally butt-butting at the handle. He reckoned that there should be approximately twenty-five different dimensions of vision, and yet he felt that it was enough that a day be divided into only three parts. That there should only be three hours in each day—the sleeping hour, the working hour and the fretting hour. He had decided that there were one hundred different degrees of drunkenness and at this moment he was in the midst of a degree eighty-four.

The Colony Astronomer didn't think much of any day.

He had got drunk watching the stars, he had got drunker fearing the stars, and he had kept drinking whilst day broke. He had sat and watched the heavens and then sat in his quarters and stared at the half-empty bottles, he had sat in the damp fog and watched the sun come up. He was maggoted—this bender had started at about ten minutes past four o' the clock the previous Thursday—and he had only just got himself asleep when someone knocked on his door. He rubbed his brow and he scoured his face and he sought to bring routine to his eyeballs. It seemed his whole body was made out of griffin claws. They knocked again. He covered his nakedness with a blanket at hand and then he opened his door sixteen and three-quarter inches and he slid himself out and presented himself upon his porch. His visitor was the Young Convict Girl Becky.

The Colony Astronomer had been rather fond of the Young Convict Girl Becky when they first boarded the Good Frigate *Ohio*, but she had soon formed a friendship with the

Colony Geologist (snippy little idler and braggart that he was), and when the Astronomer was transferred to the good ship *Furphy* under the command of Captain MacEwan she eventually drifted away from his circumstances though she did not stray from his thoughts. '*What did she want?*' He stood on his porch and he belched and he noted items of his clothing thrown madly about, strewn stray and wildly, his socks and shoes upon the path, his shirt on the step, his trousers cast off and into the Jungle, and he wondered at the manner by which he had undressed the night before. He then remembered that he was in company. It was the Convict Girl Becky. He had a notion that he had someplace heard that she was now involved with one of the soldiers, a fantastically cast human being who looked like he could plait logs. But now here she was, standing on his doorstep, grinning like a puppy.

'I think it is a good day for washing and drying. I have done all the laundry I can find, can I attend to your sheets?'

'Good God, Woman.' He said. 'Go away.'

He then retreated into his house and closed his door and watched her through the window. He was concealed by a coarse grey blanket he had nailed to the frame, she was revealed by a small hole in the top right corner where it met the nail and had been stretched and been sundered. He saw her sit down by his gate and pull mind-absently at the foliage, threading petals as she whistled. She rolled up her sleeves, she shook the dust from her skirts, she fed seeds to the grasshoppers. A kurrapuuk wandered by and squawked at her for a while and she whistled to it for a moment and chatted to it for a spell and then pointed in the direction of the Astronomer's Cabin. '*By Jesus.*' Thought the Colony Astronomer and he abandoned the window and sat upon the edge of his bed. '*He could not let this woman see his sheets.*' He thought. '*Was she mad?*' Further than that My Lord, he could not let this woman see the inside of his house, see his quarters, his room, his bed.

He had done his utmost to remove himself from the society of that colony, to extricate himself from all humanity, sleeping whilst they were at work, waking and working while they were abed.[2] She could not come in here and note the condition of his quarters. He had been a recluse for nigh on six months and felt it unfair that he should now suddenly be expected to publicly display the fell world he had created. To cast his door open to the world and invite each person's censure.

It wasn't fair. He was going mad in this insane land and this was the one small place he could come to escape. It was within these walls that he hid himself away, to drink wine and smoke tobacco, to discuss with himself the events and mysteries and machinations of the day, to laugh at his idle thoughts and weep at his sad thoughts, to scream, grin, mourn

---

[2] Governor Rantallion was outraged when the Colony Astronomer advanced that he should work these nightfall hours; he held it hinted at Jacobite intrigue, of sly and bloody insurrection. The Governor was soon able to see sense in the circumstance.

and roar, to drink and feast and smoke and to collapse in despair; the place was a pigsty. This was his holy sanctuary in the vast infernos of a living Hell on Earth; he did not come here to do housework. He came here to scream and shudder and strive to keep himself sane. There was not a horizontal surface that did not have ash or empty bottles or empty demijohns or bile upon it, there was not a vertical surface free from smoke stains or cobwebs or splashes of wine or fist holes. The smell was another thing altogether. There were his wonderful and terrible drawings lying all about everywhere. He could not have the Convict Girl Becky attend his sheets, why he hadn't seen them for five months. They had become so soiled and sodden and fetid with mould and ash and sweat and his thrilled spillage that he had ripped them from the bed last July and hidden them in some place where they had fast been covered with rubbish. He had spent these last months curling up on the rancid bare mattress, some nights in his night shirt, some nights bare and some nights fully clothed, and covered with the thin foul blanket, and willing that he might die in his sleep. He could still hear her whistling.

'You really should go. There is no reason for you to be here. Forget my sheets, forget my laundry, find other.' He said as he stood beside her and cowered and shivered before the harsh sunshine and coughed phlegm into his palm. She replied,

'You know what's happening tomorrow?'

'No, I have no idea what's happening tomorrow.' He answered and then he added, 'Nor yesterday.' And then he looked up at her for a moment and was profoundly discombobulated by her nymph-shaming beauty. He forgot himself in a grin, a brilliant grin, and he blinked his eyes and studied the ground shyly; he must look anywhere but at this girl's wonderful face. He looked down at his hands and for a moment he watched his thumbnails fiercely attack the nails of their companions, then he looked away and he glanced up at the sun. That was sufficient to tear asunder any small vestige of sobriety there was left in the fellow and he staggered for a moment, reeling blindly from its punch, and was about to tumble but for the support of the prettily and amply freckled arm of the Young Convict Girl Becky who took his shoulder and steadied him and then studied him for a moment and then asked,

'Are you not well?'

He staggered, and she let him lean his body against hers and he rested his head on her shoulder and rested his lips and his hips against her cheeks and munificent pudendum respectively. There is something about being in such close proximity to a woman that can set a drunken man's mind a-thinking. It had been nigh on nineteen months since the Astronomer had been about the merriment with a woman and he suddenly remembered why the activity was so highly esteemed, suddenly noticed that he missed the affair considerably. 'What's happening tomorrow?' he asked with a languorous whisper as he stealthily nubbed his lips against her earlobes and with his gentle fingertips wiped his sweat and his phlegm through her locks.

'You're not going along now to Jack Robinson's then?'

'No, I really hadn't thought to.' He said, as his hands pressed and fussed and searched wildly about her clothing, finding themselves atangled in her dress and many petticoats, and, when finally free and untrammelled by garmentry, repelled by her tightly clenched thighs.

'Actually I thought maybe I might just... go and have a sit by the creek back, back away from the town, if you're shy of company?' He said and he traced his fingers upon her neck and face and he sucked sweet wisps of her hair in his mouth, he kept his eyes fixed upon her splendid and proud bosom and she answered,

'Had you thought maybe you might wander over to Jack Robinson's?' Whilst striking his wet hands and wet lips away from her person.

'No, sorry I... I'm sorry, I hadn't... no I hadn't thought I would, no I do not think I will.'

'Not go to Jack Robinson's now?'

'I wouldn't imagine so. And I do beg your pardon. Why, is there a meeting?'

'There is a gentleman's discussion being conducted.'

'Oh really? Should I be there? Need I be there? Thank you.'

'It might make things better for a man.'

'I do not follow.'

'Might make things better for tomorrow.'

'Very well but in which manner, how?'

'Lord, I don't know, seems you want me to spell this thing out to you and I'm sorry but no one taught me my letters.' She said and then suddenly reeled her head aside as if it had been clonked, she crossed her eyes and said, 'Dong' and then her eyes blundered around dazedly like she was watching a fly settle on her nose. She composed herself and marshalled a more dignified mien whilst retaining a big joyful grin. The Astronomer had forgotten how talented Becky was at these unexpected shows of pantomime and he smiled fit to explode.

'No, you don't need to spell it out for me.' He clarified. 'Just stop talking in such half-thoughts, I do not associate with people enough to know what should go in the gaps you leave in your conversation.'

'I'm offering myself to tend your sheets.'

'Please, do not change the subject.'

'I do not, Sir.'

'Well then surely my thinking you had just shows how completely all at sea I am in this conversation.'

'You are a member of the Governor's colonial administration and consequently superior to a military officer.'

'My Boots you Shrew, deny that you change the subject.'

'I think well of you.'

'For God's sakes then quick, woman, tell me what you wish to say.'

'Go to Jack Robinson's.'

'By Heavens then I shall. Can you tell me why?'

'They are billeting the women.'

He returned to his quarters and hurriedly claimed his coat and trousers, hat and tobacco and coin purse and then found his faux spectacles under a pile of his wonderful and terrible pictures and he secured his door. He stood for a moment and checked his pockets for his keys and tobacco and coin purse and checked his nose for his faux spectacles, stood there by Becky, them both by the small low gate where the grass whipped at their boots, where the nettles clawed at their ankles.

'They are doing the what to the whom?' He asked.

'Just go there.' She replied.

And the Colony Astronomer complied and he raced over to Jack Robinson's quarters where he bounded up the steps to the porch and knocked on the door sharply, so sharply in fact that the sound was an abomination, an unholy uproar and he frantically tried to smother the unexpectedly terse knocks by pressing his shoulder and other arm against the door. The door was not snibbed and consequently it yielded before the Astronomer's attentions and he found himself no longer leaning against a door trying to stifle a tatty *'knock knock knock'* but falling into a room and descending towards a floor. The Astronomer hoped he had successfully concealed from the Convict Girl Becky how terribly drunk he was, by falling through the door and whacking his head on the table leg he had undoubtedly made his condition known to all the fellows there assembled. He was horribly drunk, it was two o'clock in the afternoon and he'd been on this bender for quite some time. It had been beer in his belly all day, he had drunk scotch to warm himself whilst he watched the stars, red wine to keep himself awake until morning, and rum to see in the dawn. There was pewter in his eyeballs, the inside of his mouth had started to splinter. He was bumbling around with salt on his paws, needles on his tongue, wire in his cheeks, and his brain was well sunk in brine. Falling through Jack Robinson's door and hitting his head on the furniture did little to assist his situation. It was beyond him to stand up in this warworn condition so instead he bundled up his stray limbs and curled up below the table.

'You're early drunk, Mr Casey, I see. Half your bloody luck.' Said Captain Harman. 'We were about billeting the women.'

The Astronomer curled up under Jack Robinson's table, rested his head on a cushion somebody had generously passed down to him, and settled into listening to the murmur of their voices. They were talking about a situation in which certain women were put in the lascivious service of certain gentlemen. He could not follow the story. He recognised the occasional familiar name but he would have thought that these were names from a somehow different story. No—the names and the story were complementary. Yes—this was a story about men being bequeathed bed-whores. And yes—it was going to take place with names he knew. It was going to take place here. Here in Old & New Bridgeford! The *what* was going to take place here in Old & New Bridgeford? The thing about the bequeathing of the women. He was really going to have to concentrate. Was he privy to a great scandal or on the other hand totally misunderstanding what was going on around him?

'I'll have the fiery Portsmouth whore called Char-Duck.' Said Old Captain Bridewell. turning abruptly in his chair and lewdly adjusting his genitals before the Astronomer's face.

'No, I'm sorry, Captain Bridewell.' Said Captain Harman. 'We have talked to the sparky red-head called Char-Duck. She has taken a fancy to the Second to the Quarter-Master and she will not have a bar of you.'

Yes it was going on the way he'd thought it. The Astronomer listened and listened as they talked and talked and he was astonished by what he heard. His fellows were bargaining for harlots. He had to get out of here. Billeted? What a sweet euphemism Corporal Harman and Becky had reckoned up when they used the term billeted, thought the Astronomer, for what we had here, in no uncertain terms, was a god-forsaken slave auction. Woe, this was mad debauchery. He couldn't move.

He had never heard of the plan to allocate certain of the convict women to the quarters of certain of the men, he had never studied a precedent, he was anxious that the whole contrivance reeked of barbarity, of slavery, of bloody tyranny, he was vainfully trying to impose order upon his thoughts. He was intrigued by the plan's considerable promise. He was concerned and bothered and ill-footed and when he learnt that he would be allowed a selection he was terrified and vexed and anxious.

'You know, of course, dear William.' Said Rotund Jack Robinson, prodding the Astronomer's head with the toe of his boot, and whispering below the table. '... You know of course that you're entitled to a selection Mr Casey.'

It was too extreme to comprehend. He was to be allowed a mistress? A slave girl? An attendant, hand-picked, hand-chosen and free to be handled? Could he have seven? He couldn't believe it. Here he could choose his bed-wench? Out here in this faraway land beyond the survey of England's cold tyranny and laws and edicts and censure? Like some magnificent Sultan he was to be allowed a concubine? Perchance a seraglio from this mad imbroglio? How enthralling. He could deem it so? And did all of this tie in with that strange conversation he had just had with the Convict Girl Becky? She clearly knew of this matter, but she was keeping company with Sergeant Salt, what was she conspiring at? It defied comprehension, it was beyond his reckoning, he declined immediately.

'Why goodness no, Jack. I am... quite attendant to my quarters and have not felt the want of company. I am... my nights of work, my days of rest would mark me a very poor companion. And My Word, I have a dear wife in England to whom I am married.'

'Your commission and the sea voyage place her four years and eight months shy of this place. She's on another planet, chum.'

'But I...'

'It's a long time to milk your turnip. You can either pipe up now or you can forever hold your peace. Still, that's your decision...' Said Jack Robinson and they both turned their attention to the conversation of their fellows.

'Sergeant Salt is out at New Bridgeford these four days.' Said Captain Harman. 'But he requested that I place dibs on the one called Becky.'

The Astronomer had resolutely refused at first but such a speech by Captain Harman was sufficient to throw such resolution awry. He ordered his thoughts and then made his point backwards.

'But is my rank not superior to Sergeant Salt's?' He said, straightening his cuffs and correcting his collar and clipping his buttons and sitting himself quickly upright and hitting his head on the underside of the table.

''Tis how the Governor has seen fit to arrange it.'

'I have noticed how you have sorted out the disputes in this matter.' Said the Astronomer organising himself out from under the table and leaning himself up against the wall. 'Does not a twice-esteemed girl go to the man of higher rank?' He said stumbling.

'That's the case.'

'Well there it is.'

'I beseech you Mr Casey, please remember you are drunk, Sir and must make mightier efforts to ensure your comments are intelligible.'

'Oh, I'll eventually be intelligible.'

'Speed it up, Sir.'

'Perhaps, were a man of my rank to think fondly of this girl called Becky, would he not in this instance have the precedent claim, would he?'

Chapter 14   The Convict Girl Becky

The Astronomer thought very fondly of the girl called Becky and so should we all. She was a captivating little jumping bean. She had astonishingly dun hair, it seethed like oil, it welled in deep pools of fearsome darkness. It was cut short, neatly cropped for fear of nits, a clumsy and nasty hurried disarray of hair which did very little to recommend the quality of her locks, but sure revealed and fast drew one's attention to her splendid, splendid neck. She was beauty my word, she was bitchin'. She had storms of pale slight freckles that seemed to move and shift upon her skin, that welled and whirled across her cheeks and dusted down her neck and floated on her ample bust. These freckles reappeared from beneath her cuffs and below her hemline. They revealed nothing of the journey they had taken beneath her clothing from the neckline to the cuff and cloth line except that they hinted that there may be an abundance of their counterparts still abay beneath her clothing. Small delightful fairy-circles of freckles, and rich, caramel and chocolate raised-up ones all clustered and scattered all over her creamy skin, all over her brilliant body.

Her pleasing aspect framed a pair of pale cloudy green eyes, sleepy and languid eyes, that jumped about and darted about like a pair of wicked sprites, they were forever aflight and alive, pale dusty green and incessantly in motion, they were like the mould you'd get on fire. It was clear that this woman was dwelling upon madness; both addressing it with great scrutiny and finding it her firmament—she was a firecracker. Four years spent as her partner would be a carnival ride indeed—part balloon trip, part rodeo horse.

CHAPTER 15

Oh Yes, the Colony Astronomer thought very fondly of this girl called Becky and truth be told he thought very often of this girl called Becky. Why it was she who had started off the whole wonderful and terrible drawing thing initially. It was her beauty that he had sought to capture a thousand times, her likeness that he had caught upon the page and then embellished with his pencil. And it was her beauty that had led him to defer from detailing his subject's clothing and first saw him depict his subject naked.

The Colony Astronomer, like our friend the Colony Botanist, had set himself the task of rendering likenesses of his compatriots. When they had landed in this place the nature of his duties had allowed him free hours each day to fill at his whim and he had taken his pencil to his page and sketched many portraits of his fellows. He had drawn himself up a thousand sketches of these people as he sat himself beneath a tree and watched them about their duties. Drawn pictures of the Sailmaster Hopkins as he folded skillfully, the Cardsmaster Meister as he folded artfully, and the Linen Char Peggy as she folded menially. He had drawn himself pictures of Becky. Studied her face and copied it craftfully. Noted her bonnet and dutifully depicted her hands and the beads of sweat upon her forearms, detailed her cleavage and hinted her blouse. Etched in her face, faithfully rendered each freckle and rich luscious mole, each lash and muscle, and then vaguely suggested her garmentry. The cloth, the collars, the cuffs and the crinoline he would sketch in at night, each evening filling in the extraneous details of the bib to the fore and the branches in the background. And, fatefully, there came a night when he deferred further the detailing of Becky's clothing but rather speculated upon the naked situation of her bosom, reckoned up the curve of her naked back, the slender sweep of her naked thigh, the gentle forest of her pubis. Then he drew himself up hundreds of pictures of the Convict Girl

Becky unhampered by crude dress, untrammelled by unforgiving corsetry and bind, underwearing underwear, and naked and free and pure beneath the sun, intricately touched between the legs, cross-hatched and shaded. After a month and with the aid of his mirror and pencil he drew himself into these same pictures. Alone and at night he had sat by his desk and considered her beauty and had imagined the sight of their congress, and his able right hand with pencil clutched had proven the good companion of his imaginings. He had drawed himself a hundred sketches of himself and the Convict Girl Becky about their business and he treasured each and every one of them. He had spent many a night curled up under his blanket and considered her beauty and considered the possibilities of their congress and again found that his able right hand was a good companion to his imaginings. And none of his imaginings had shown her being sired by that Piece of Dry Bull's Gristle Sergeant Salt. Four years and eight months was a long time to milk his turnip, it was a lifetime. He either spoke now or forever held his piece. He would have his Becky.

The Astronomer vomited into his hat and then he straightened himself up and rubbed the back of his hand across his mouth and prepared himself for Captain Harman's rejoinder.

'What's your point?'

'Merely, that I think well of the girl called Becky.'

And he poured himself a scotch.

Chapter 16

The Colony Astronomer sat desolutely upon his poor derelict bed pulling absent-mindedly on stray, torn bits of padding that were poking out from the cushions upon which he sat.

He fretted in his cabin and he chewed his nails and he considered the events of that afternoon and he surveyed his surroundings. He had won, boldly won. He was a member of the Governor's interim administration and hence he had been able to compel the Convict Girl Becky in service. Becky was to be his housemate. Sergeant Salt was going to have to stew in his own juices because from now on it would be the Astronomer who was going to be stewing in hers. *'Hah.'* Said the Astronomer *'Good one.'* He said as he took a bitter swig from his bottle of Jack Robinson's gin and then he said, *'Oh Hell.'*

'She was to come here?' *'She couldn't live here.'* *'What was he going to do?'* He wondered, as he considered the empty bottles and half-remembered meals and abandoned rolls of tobacco, the sordid sorry ruins of his small solitary kingdom. He couldn't bring her here. He shook his head aghast at the scale of his dilemma. He was going to have to move. He was going to have to burn this place down and move to pristine quarters but, alas, there were no pristine quarters to be had. 'No, I am beset by a worse fate.' Thought the Astronomer. 'I'm going to have to tidy up.'

He did not want to tidy up, he couldn't be bothered. He didn't want to. Things had gone too far. There was just too much mess. There was no escaping this smell. Oh, he couldn't burn off all this wretched nonsense, he had not been seen to start a bonfire in the six months they'd been arrest in this place, were he to do so it would surely invite comment. Oh yes, he could just see himself starting a fire to burn the rubbish and the wretched wonderful drawings. Not much happened to divert the attention in Old & New Bridgeford, were he to suddenly start a bonfire he would soon have an audience of six hundred. He could bury the bottles, he could hoe into the soil the rotten food, he didn't know what he could do with his bloody pictures. The ones of him and Becky about their fanciful couplings, the one of the convict wench Carutthers passing her water, the sketches of the Spanish Girl, the one of her caught wet in her garmentry the day of the sudden storm, her calico shirt sheer against her chest, her nipples roused and stirred and affronted by the sudden cold, the sketches of dear wondrous Becky about her bath, with her shirt low or shed, her nipples taut and perky, her nethers cool, alluring and enticing. There were so many pictures, the ribald ones, the rude and lewd, the ones that lampooned, the one of Captain Bridewell, depicted in all his soldierly finery and yet drawn by the Colony Astronomer trying to piss into his own mouth. The picture of the Colony Governor with the ears and snout of a mule and the member of that same creature, the one of Sergeant Salt with the character and cast of a kitten, the sketch of the Colony Cartographer trembling and timorous and playing the mistress to his shrewish belle. So many of these illustrations were comical and libellous, they were intended to amuse the Astronomer—*Everybody is aware that the priest is seeking favours from the boy lag Fletcher, see them here about their commerce*—*Everyone knows that Stench of Cum Shanker is very fond of his proud whistle, here he finds it in a most astonishing place.* And sometimes they were decidedly raunchy, they were intended to arouse the Astronomer—*Here is the Convict Girl Becky, see how the light filters through her shirt allowing us to consider her fine bosom, see here how the Astronomer laps upon her quim.* He could not have any person seeing these drawings, and if any person, God not, most not, Becky. Were he to cache them they would be found, if he should burn them he would have a thousand spectators. He had to get rid of his pictures. He had to drown them in a swampy bog, bury them in a skein of tree roots, he had to drop them in a bottomless hole.

So he gathered all his pictures, his mad and depraved lustful imaginings of his company and he bundled them all up in sacks and bags and secreted them out into the night. He crept down to the military stables and commandeered a horse. He refused to reveal his reasons when challenged by the Corporal on watch duty. He put a gun to the fellow's head and then rode off madly into the night.

He rode for miles, he rode for dozens of miles and he raced his horse across the plains of stone, he urged his horse through the thick and dense bush, he made it bridge the creeks and he made it ford the billabongs. He rode for hours and he found that there was not a swampy bog, not a skein of tree roots, nor a bottomless hole to be had. He rode until he could ride no further, the conclusion not due to any great exhaustion on his part or that of his horse but enforced by his reaching a ruddy great precipice. A great cut in the land that stretched beyond the eye could see on either side, left bare air before him and saw the resumption of the land some eight thousand feet below.

The country beyond all looked the same and ordered like that land about him, it was just that it was eight thousand feet lower, somebody had allowed this country to drop untidily, and nobody had been bothered to set it right. He knew that his compatriots made their home some two thousand miles to the West on the coast that was mapped by the Dutchmen. Between this point where he stood then and the land of New Holland he knew there was this great mass of emptiness, a vast unknown world. When he reached the mighty cliff that forbade further travel he gathered up the sacks and bags and rolls of his wonderful and dreadful drawings, held them up high above his head and screamed out, 'In pity, Dear Lord, then let me be free' and then he heaved them beyond the known realm of man, into that great well of oblivion, into the vast hole of nothingness where they landed in the summer hunting grounds of the Kennilang Tribe who gathered them all up and fast re-secured them and promptly returned them to the white tribe they'd seen making camp on the shore to the East.

They arrived shyly at first, tossing a few sticks and rocks about the bush to declare their arrival and, having assembled a crowd, they waved their spears above their heads, their woomeras and boomerangs, and they held up some dirty sacks and they screeched. They threw the sacks down upon the ground and clicked their heavy sticks at them and kicked dust upon them. They danced in circles and hooted merrily.

This was a first, an astonishing first, in the history of diplomacy. Never before in the bold history of mankind had a civilisation chosen to introduce itself to another in the manner selected by the English when meeting the Kennilang people. We have all, as time has progressed and the world has indeed become a village, eventually learnt of each other's pornography. We have all become aware of the paintings and sculptures and erotica that each other has, during the centuries, used to titillate ourselves. When the French signed a treaty with the Turks in a bay by Constantinople it was not long before the Turks learnt of the lewd etchings of Mr Chauvet and the depraved sketches of François Boucher, and even sooner was a French sailor offered 'feelthy pictures' by an enterprising Turk. When Richard the Lionheart looted the infidel's grand libraries, he read the Koran and accounted their maps during the day, he studied 'The Scented Garden' into the wee hours of the night. When Western man met the Japanese they traded porcelain and herbs and gold and gunpowder, the works of Kitagawa Utamaro were swapped for those of Borel and Elluin. Englishmen titter at the pet names in 'The Karma Sutra', Mexicans chortle at the paintings of de Ghent and Romberg, Chinamen can laugh at the ambitious penises of Touko Laaksonen the Finn, we can all concede the arousing lyricism of Courbet's 'Origin of the World' and dismiss as far too strenuous the practices of the black and orange gentlemen on old Grecian jars. As each civilisation has gradually become more intricately and inexplicably entwined we have all eventually encountered each other's erotica and whilst we may laugh at the occasional obsession, variation or gaucheness, we can all delight in the occasionally splendid whimsy of each other's fetishes, note relievedly that we have all developed some local variety of homosexuality, sado-masochism, pornography itself and the quaffing of urine, and all release a pent-up sigh of relief when we realise that at least each and everyone else of us finds the entire affair wholly confusing.

As I say, this process has usually been gradual, part of a progressive and yet dynamic exchange of information, culture and ideas. This was the first time, here to the West of Old & New Bridgeford between the Kennilang people and the English people that it had been done out and out first thing off the block.

It was certainly an irregular moment in the history of cultural exchange and it required a great deal of generosity from the Kennilang people to excuse the Englishmen's considerable faux pas. And they tried at first. They walked timidly amongst the white people and pointed this or that one out to the other and covered their smiles with their hands. They giggled at this one here and then stifled the giggle and contained their mirth. 'What on earth are they laughing at?' Wondered the white folk as the Colony Astronomer desperate fought his way through their number, keeping a wild eye on those sacks. It was the sight of the Cartographer and the woman Megsy that unfortunately broke the resolve of the Kennilang people.

There was one amongst their company who was considerably older then his fellows, he wore a fine yellow headband and it was he who carried the sacks. He was part mystic, part tribal elder, part sage and, more importantly, he was the first one amongst them who could sober up after a laugh and explain a situation,

'Nirrum Chubbay.' He said to the Cartographer. 'Nirrum Chubbay, ey? Gottum finder et nem bendey bendey, ey, nif wanna nif wanna, ey. Doot nay em finnum?'

'You never mind them.' He said to the Cartographer. 'They have seen the pictures of you and this woman about your commerce. They're thinking that each of you has mistaken themself for the other person, you are the fella right?'

The Astronomer was now within reach of the Indians and was trying desperately to grab those sacks. The Second to the Quarter-Master and the Portsmouth Whore had made their way to the fore of the crowd gathered around the Indians and their arrival was greeted with effusive mirth on the part of the dark-skinned people until Old Man Yellow Headband shook his head and sighed and knocked his knuckles against the Second to the Quarter-Master's chest and said,

'*Graat Walla fortem. Graat Walla fortem. Nay liffdem ay mindum ey Kookaburra Waw Waw Waw Waw. Do bella milutty liftum?*'

'Hello to you two. These stupid kids laugh to see what is only natural between a man and a woman. You pay them no accord, you just tell me how you got yourself that fellow the size of a piccaninny's arm?'

'Good Lord. What's the affair?' Said Governor Rantallion making his way through the mass of sundry convicts and standing beside the Colony Astronomer who was now frantically grasping at the sacks and had indeed claimed one which he had secured to the ground with his firmly planted foot and the old native said,

'*Goot nay for da pluttener.* Oh yours is a long thin snake, my friend. What is it, are you forgetting to feed him?' And to Sergeant Salt he leant forward and whispered,

'*Oh gunna et do nosun, nofurrah, nofurrah denown.* Hello to the fellow with the witchetty grub for a member. Tell me, why do you direct attentions to the woman of this fellow He-Grabs-at-Bags. In our tribe we do not allow bigamy, though it is practised by the Gaddiwalla tribe who live to the South.' And then he turned to the Governor and put his fingers to his lips and he nibbled at the air before them. Governor Rantallion said,

'Yes that's it. He's got the right idea. This fellow wants food, find some food for the man. Get him bread and water, bring him cheese and some ham, show him a potato and fetch the jar of pickled octopus from my quarters. That'll set his toes tapping.'

And Old Man Yellow Headband settled back comfortably upon his legs and rhythmically drummed his fingers upon his potbelly and smiled beatifically. And the Governor said,

'Yes take him somewhere and sate this fellow and learn a few of his words. Teach him some of ours. Explain our presence here and the Monarchy and how we are about at things, and of Agincourt and the Crusades and our adventures in India and Africa and China, and that bastard Washington, and assure him that we shall not molest him. Now promptly, I must see what is in these bags.'

And the troop of Indians were led away to the Quarter-Master's Tent accompanied by the greater part of the people who had gathered and been watching these strange affairs unfold, and who were intent upon observing the spectacle of these particular and wonderful people eating. A few of the other folk remained behind and heard the by now profoundly panicky Colony Astronomer say,

'These bags contain belongings of mine.'

'Are you sure, Mr Casey?' Inquired the Governor. 'These people have carried them a very long way.'

'They are mine, Sir, let me take them, Sir, they are mine.'

'But I should not sleep an easy night if I did not know their contents. They are clearly new to this land, if they are yours well and good but if they are not we must be alarmed at a European presence so close to our village.'

'I tell you, Sir, they are mine, let me have them, why don't you just let me...' Said the Colony Astronomer and the Governor replied,

'And still, Sir, I will see their contents.'

And those standing about remembered the mystery of the Astronomer's strange behaviour and were likewise fast eager to know the contents of the Astronomer's lost sacks. Captain Naskin and the Colony Rat Catcher, Jack Robinson butt-butted the tobacco from his pipe and moved closer to the Governor, the Spanish Girl, and the Second to the Quarter-Master, and the Convict Girl Becky, all shouldered in next to the Governor as he drew his knife from its scabbard and then placed the blade against the stubborn cloth.

'They are clearly European, if they are yours well and good but I shall still see their contents.'

And he roughly jostled the point of the knife through the coarse cloth, wrenched the knife upwards causing the blade to further impair the material and then set upon slicing and sawing at the hessian. The blade suddenly reared upwards and allowed all watchers a split-second, vague and momentary glimpse of the dark interior, of some papers and pages and illustrations. The Colony Astronomer gasped. Governor Rantallion called for the assistance of the Colony Tailor who had upon his person a pair of hardy scissors.

'Then I beg you, Sir.' Said the Colony Astronomer. 'May it be done in private.'

'Oh yes, very well. Let's you and me do it inside.'

And the Governor and the Colony Astronomer and the sacks disappeared behind the Governor's closed door and those few left in their wake spat angrily in the dust, they shook their heads and felt crossly that these affairs had not met their expectations. They were then eager to return to their duties and were resolved that they could never be distracted a third time when the colony's resident member of the indigenous population, a fellow called Our Bennelong called their bluff:

'I know that fella's words. You never believe what he's been saying. You'd never think of the drawings that Starfellas drawn up and got himself inside that sack.'

And they all stopped to listen.

Part III

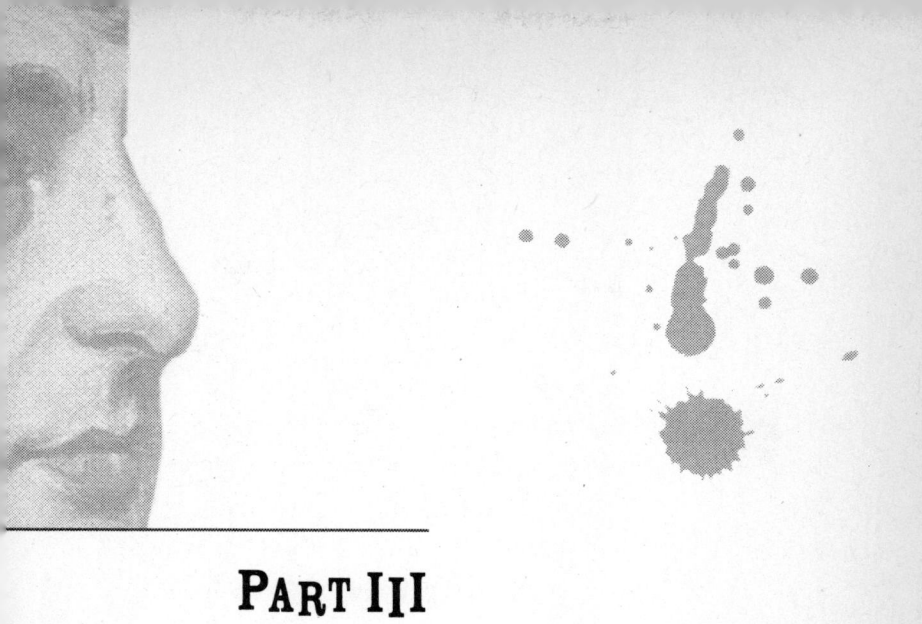

CHAPTER 17

Governor Rantallion stood to the fore of the back of the sideless stage that constituted the temporary courthouse and he coughed into the palm of his left hand and then with his right he picked a bit of tobacco from his lower lip, he then scratched the tip of his nose and then said the following to anyone who was within ear shot which proved to be every person of the colony who had there been assembled for the purpose of hearing this address, whilst ridding his left hand of its phlegmy cargo by rubbing it on the underside of the rostrum behind which he stood.[3]

'Well, then, Good Afternoon all.' He orated. 'Yes, make yourself comfortable you few stragglers. Now. I do not think there is one person of us at all unclear upon our point in being here in Old & New Bridgeford at home in this new and strange

---

[3] Everyone except of course for that thatch of soldiers over at New Bridgeford who included among their company Sergeant Salt certainly, and the Galley Cook and the Cacklesmith probably; John Dunnock was absent of course, as was Doctor Wilmot possibly.

land. Yes, we are here to etch the faint name of England upon the dust. Now that six months have elapsed and we have humbled up a few small huts and crude buildings, erected this fine flag pole and scrambled up some docks, now that six months have elapsed and we have gloriously and honourably declared unequivocally Great England's slight and vague ill-defined interest in this land, let us strike ourselves down a home. We have done what Mother England requires of us, enough of us are still alive and this flag can be seen from the sea, now let us do what our souls require of us. Let us make ourselves a land. Let us build ourselves here upon this hillside an honest village, nay a fair and proud town, a stately city, no let us build for the delight of the o'erlooking Cosmos, here in these Antipodes, a mighty Metropolis. That in two hundred years' time, when people consider upon our exploits, they shall think they speak of great and mighty deeds. Let us build our houses two storeys high, let us pave the roads and light the streets and roll our fields out like proud carpets. Let us ford the streams with rocks and bridge the rivers with stone, let us master the mountains and raze the forests and reap the coal fields and filigree our doors with gold. Let us strike our names upon the firmament.

'Gentleman of this Colony, I call upon you all to untether your great talents, let you spare no moment, master each challenge and rise to great levels of achievement.

'Ladies, I call upon you to not err nor slacken in your great industry and ingenuity.

'We all eat poorly here, our provisions are meagre, but for those of you prisoners here who show themselves capable of a day's honest work there shall be an eighth extra rations and there shall be rest days.

'To assist in this great purpose... this fine and noble purpose... I have always intended that with the passage of six months, certain of the women prisoners who have shown themselves to be of good and repentant character... can you hear up the back there?... Shown they to be trustworthy and commendable, should be allowed a greater liberty about this our home and should perform house and garden service to certain gentlemen of the colony. By this situation I hope these gentlemen shall find more hours to pursue their great duties—to reckon the stars, tide and winds, the inhabitants, fauna and plants of this land and let the women tend the linen and the pumpkins, let the women tend the roads and the shires and the accidents and disputes.

'Accordingly, let any man who has a word to speak upon this affair please state his thoughts.'

Young Corporal Robertson had a word to speak upon the affair and he did so kneeling, keening and crawling in the dust and clutching to the hem of the Governor's coat.

'I beg you Sir, let the Spanish Convict transported for stealing the end off a plaice, for being a gypsy and for distributing insurrectionary pamphlets be assigned to my service in the bunk house, or to your quarters, or to the quarters of any good person about this colony except those of Captain Naskin and God No not back to the women's quarters.'

'Excuse me a moment.' Said Governor Rantallion, 'Dear Jack, you have an interest in this matter.'

And Jack Robinson chuckled and re-tucked his shirt into his trousers and said, 'Yes, I've an avowed interest. I've taken a *liken* to a Larkin.' And he stated his cause and Pitt the Judge Advocate made his arguments and the Colony Banker advanced his interests and the Colony Tailor explained his point and the Colony Porter pushed his case.

Affairs proceeded generally in the manner that had been expected—the Second to the Quarter-Master commanded the service of the Portsmouth Whore called Char-Duck, the tawny-haired lass Linda Thomas was to attend to the quarters of the Governor, the pickpocket Megsy was billeted to the Cartographer. The occasion proceeded perhaps in the manner of an election night where the result is well expected and widely anticipated and all the intrigue and drama is played out in the odd and unexpected electoral seat. The Colony Botanist astonished every person of that town when he called for the service of the defaulting fencer of gate stakes, Young Peg Welch. The Colony Astronomer startled them all when he appeared and loudly stated his point and counter-point and conclusive point-of-rebuttal and then, having sufficiently bewildered them all with his drunken and mad rantings, he promptly departed. The Colony Bakers got into a bunfight. Of course, Young Robertson was a surprise and constant entertainment; Young Corporal Robertson, that most shy, earnest and proper of young gentlemen, was quite a sight as he roared and gnashed his teeth and cast dust into the air and beat his fists upon his chest and his head upon the ground.

'What unholy horror has here been wrought?' cried Young Corporal Robertson. He had committed his beloved to the care of the most evil man his nineteen years of varied experience had seen him encounter. He had saved her from violence and abuse he had, but my God, what perils did that sanctuary harbour. She was to go into the lair of Captain Naskin nightly and there to fend for herself. Out of the frying pan into the fire was right, straight there into the Damned Fires of Hell. He had forever agreed with the Colony Dentist and the Provost Marshall and the wretched Colony Cartographer when they had reckoned that there would be temporary salvation for the Spanish Girl if she were billeted to the safe quarters of some good gentleman of the colony. It was a wise and prosperous thought, but woe he was horrified and aghast on that morning when the Colony Cartographer suggested that Captain Naskin might be that same fellow. He immediately gave protest and only was silent when they pulled rank and commanded that their will be so and even then it was an insurrectionary silence for he wept and swore constantly, he moaned and feverishly mumbled loud prayers that they reconsider.

He had not once abandoned the importunate hope that affairs may develop unexpectedly to the contrary, that an alternative course might be found and he did not abandon that desperate hope for the duration of the Governor's speech nor during the billeting of the women that followed.

'Please let the Spanish Girl be taken from the women's quarters, Oh Noble Governor, but let it be to my quarters or to the quarters of Father Pittman or let her be called First Nurse of the Infirmary or allow yourself an extra housekeeper, just let her not go into the Den of Captain Naskin.'

I shall spare you the sad details of those scenes, spare you the distress of observing Young Robertson's tears and anguished cries as he thrashed about in the dust at the Governor's feet, I shall not disturb your comfort by describing the pain, horror and despair that o'erwracked the Spanish Girl when she reckoned with her predicament and then collapsed lifelessly to the ground. The salty tears that welled and flowed from Robertson's enchanting and boyish blue eyes, the fearful beating of her proud and ample bosom knowing that these sad affairs may well provoke tears from some reader of kind and gentle heart, some dear and tender soul and knowing that, as affairs ultimately pan out, they are events that one is best to consider with the advantage of hindsight.

All you need note is that Governor Rantallion gave no attention to Young Robertson's earnest suit, nor was any counter-suit made by any other person and the Spanish Girl was soon amongst those poor convicts being rounded up by the soldiers and who would soon be marched and herded away and despatched and directed to their duties.

It was only then, after all the deals had been struck—after all the assignations and associations and appointments, annointments and disappointments had been wrought—that a few of those there convicts looked about their number and looked at those that had left their company and then looked back at the other *'not-pickeds'* and a few of those there convicts packed up the Governor's rostrum and started stacking up the chairs.

The whores and the alleysluts and the cutthroats and the knifehearts looked at those women about themselves and then looked in upon themselves and then looked at the vast rank of lower soldiers and secondary gentlemen—those fellows who had not on this day been allocated a woman but whose fortunes still lay before them and then looked about themselves at their fellow she-lags. They looked down at their fingernails and the sharps rocks about their feet and checked the security of the contraband knives they had hidden beneath their skirts and their pleats, looked at the girls in their company, looked at the Spanish Girl amongst others, and then the Provost Marshall nudged his elbow into Captain Naskin's back and Captain Naskin hiccoughed and he stumbled having—I must apologise—momentarily dozed off and he quickly said,

'Oh and also Governor Rantallion, I shall need the Spanish Girl.'

Chapter 18   Captain Naskin and the Spanish Girl

Captain Naskin had not the faintest idea what to do with this patient and quietly expectant powder keg of humanity sitting in anticipation by his table. He usually spent these hours chewing furiously upon his fingernails. After two hours of self-consumption he would be ready to make himself a cup of tea, to shift his leg, to draw the curtains. Tonight he was required to play host to this strange and beautiful woman sitting here patiently beside him and the whole time scheming up her own plots and plans and deceptions. And tomorrow night and for quite a number of nights in the foreseeable future.

'Well... I suppose we better establish where you sleep. It's here.' He said and he ushered her to a rather pleasant looking alcove that had been hidden away behind a curtain of hessian. 'It's a strong bed but I fear you might be troubled by that sun coming up in that window. You can secure that curtain I've put up but I reckon it's still going to be mighty unfair. Sorry, it's the best I've got.' And he secured the curtain. 'Don't try any monkeying around with when you depart and when you return. There's no secret about your relationship with Robertson, I wish you both all the very best; he seems a reasonable enough fellow. I just don't wish it to be some comical pantomime all up before me do you understand? I'm a light sleeper and a keen observer, if you sneak around and try to keep secrets from me I'll know it more sharply than if it were just done out in the daylight and for all to see. Now, can you play cards?'

The Spanish Girl had barely followed the course of conversation as it had progressed; she could not for a moment shift with it when it changed tack so abruptly. She vaguely nodded and then somehow found herself playing cards.

Something should be said of the Spanish Girl at this point and that is that her language skills were terrific. She had learnt just about all she needed to know of English and she had learnt it like a duck takes to water. I tossed in that tired old thingummy-jigger just to illustrate the point, she would have known precisely what it meant and she would have known that it had very little to do with ducks. She could barter. One of the first things living in this new land England had demanded of her was that she could stake her claim in the marketplace, and she had done so like a well-lubed porpoise takes to a pool of camomile oil. She could haggle. She soon learnt that a sack of pumpkins could be traded in for a fresh chicken and she soon learnt how to ensure a few onions were added to secure the deal. She fast learnt how to talk to the policeman, how to distract the collector, how to befuddle the banker. She could feyly beg an extra week from the landlord. English was hers and she wielded it like a sweet sabre of primrose. She plunked it down on the platters of plenty and charmed the accountants. She had so mastered this foreign tongue that she was able to sculpt it into the seduction of Robertson but she'd never learnt how to use it to play cards.

It had not occurred to her to master this language in the lingo of playing cards. She had not anticipated the circumstances where it would be required and encountering them, she soon rued the neglect.

What on earth was a bower? She did not care whether it was the left one or the right one, she did not have a primary understanding of the concept. 'It is a Knave getting uppity.' She protested. She had a fairly good reckoning of the word *misère*, she understood it in the French context, she could not for a moment see how it could apply to a card game.

They spent many hours playing cards, those two of them there together, the collective endeavour allowed them to disregard their discomfort, the shared task and pleasure allowed them to relax and not note the demands of their situation, to inadvertently reveal different angles and aspects of their character. Captain Naskin proved a kind and gentle teacher; his ministrations to his pupil were ever-patient and ever-helpful. As she struggled with the rules of this strange and foreign game, as she stumbled with the words, he chuckled her along, he gently chided her errors and corrected her mistakes, he ensured she was never wanting for a fair cup of tea. He was a fine and wise teacher, he was a fearsome opponent.

'God Jesus again with the selection from my discards.'

'I thought you said I could take from there...'

'I never said you could take from there every time.'

'Well how many times can I...'

'You can take from there every bloody time if you like the card.'

'But then why are you...'

'It just matches me ill that you take from there every fucking time.'

The Spanish Girl went silent.

'You've gone silent.' Said Captain Naskin. 'Do you want to play your discard?'

'Not just at the moment, I think I shall rest my cards.'

'Well can you just cast your other and then rest your cards and let me have my shot?'

The Spanish Girl tossed her card away; Captain Naskin neglected it and he drew from the deck. He excitedly rearranged his existing cards to accommodate this promising newcomer and he said,

'You know enough of English to hold a sensible conversation. You speak the tongue surely, may I propose—not that I think you less than a gentle woman—you have learnt that there are certain words that are not fit to be spoken in the company of a lady.'

'I know of such words.'

'And "bloody" is one of them?'

'I am not fond of the word.'

'How about "fucking"?'

'I know the word does not have a gentle pedigree.'

'Then I wish it away from our conversation. I apologise for my barbarity and I thank you for your fine example. I was just becoming steadily riled by the way you were constantly picking up the cards I neglect, the way you grab them up and shuffle them into your greedy little nest like some dear merry-dew, it's beginning to...'

'This is because you are so often losing, Sir?'

'No it's not because I'm f... It must be your turn. Are you dishing upon the abundance or are you scavenging from my tossed out bones?'

The Spanish Girl looked at the *abundance* and considered the unknown promise this tight and neatly stacked order of unknown cards could yield. She had seen a dearly desired ten be discarded and swept away in the consequent bundle of debris, she was still hoping for a second. She could hold out vainly for another six or she could throw in her lot with that odd cluster of Jacks and Queens. Or she could scavenge from his tossed out bones and lo and yippity; it was a Red Ace.

You don't need to know much about this card game to get the vague gist of this poor tale—knowledge of the intriguing tallying up process by which points were deducted from the loser's score would be wildly superfluous information, however I do hold that you need a reasonable understanding of the value of a Red Ace. These buggers were dear treasure, cherished nuggets, they were the mother lode. There were only two of them and they were the very key to the game. Within the rules of this game their black brothers were hollow shadows, poor forlorn wraiths and may as well have been discarded from the pack such was the sheer power that the Ace of Hearts and the Ace of Diamonds had drawn to their chests. Carmine and sanguine they were a joy to be dealt and ever welcome. The Red Ace was the wild card, it was the glorious miracle that turned those two stray sevens into a three of a kind, that linked that awkward five and six of clubs with the eight, nine and ten up here that became a lovely run of six. These cards were eagerly sought after, they could turn a vain rabble and possibly disastrous weight of cards into a neatly ordered regiment of sprighty possibilities. The game was called 'Red Ace'. Only an idiot would discard one, an idiot or some person who has momentarily been distracted from the game. Captain Naskin had just tossed away the Ace of Diamonds.

'Do you know what you've just thrown away?' Asked the Spanish Girl.

'What? Why are you... Oh for God's sakes. Just give me a moment, that's not fair.'

'You were just addressing the circumstances by which I can select from your discards... Is it an accord on this occasion?'

'But we were all about it, Ma'am, if we start off on some almighty great a-talking it's not fair if I'm not allowed to reconsider...'

'So, I can pick it up.'

'For the sake of Jesus you were shaming me for my foul speech, I can hardly be expected to...'

'Well I think I will pick it up...'

'Rather, I should be allowed to claim it and then you should be allowed to select a card from my fractured deck and make that the... It's not fair.'

'... or would you prefer not to play anymore?'

'Sweet madam, you bring shame to the angels, you are a mother of whores.'

And then there came a ring upon Captain Naskin's bell. It was Young Corporal Robertson. He was here for his night-time calling come-a-courting thing.

Both of them seemed to freeze, the Spanish Girl with her hand hovering over that shining Red Ace, and the weary flop of tired not-*Red Aces*, Captain Naskin, because he was already still.

The Spanish Girl did not know what to do. Was she to take the Red Ace or leave it? If she took the Red Ace she knew that that would just send some message that she had taken the card for some reason, however if she left the Red Ace that would just send some other message about her for some strange reason leaving the Red Ace. She didn't know how to send the message that was tumbling and rumbling in her heart, which was that this conversation had been unfortunately interrupted. That she wished this process of outwitting each other to continue or at least she wished it to resume at some latter time at the exact point where it had left off. She wavered between taking his card and weathering the bold messages that sent out or choosing from the deck and then somehow grabbing back the strategic surrender of power that that action would inevitably constitute, she did not for a moment know what to do and the fact that Young Robertson was ringing the bell a second time made deciding that wee bit harder.

'Well we can leave the cards about in this manner. If I'm still about this evening we can finish on your return.' Said Captain Naskin and he saw himself from the table.

'Thank God for Captain Naskin.' Thought The Spanish Girl. 'Of course we should leave the cards set up. That declares firmly and surely that something has been momentarily interrupted and shall be returned to shortly. I admire your thinking.' The Spanish Girl grabbed up the Red Ace and chucked out the dinky five of spades and breezed out to see what young Robertson had to say for himself.

CHAPTER 19 ANOTHER CARD NIGHT

'He cannot win against Russia if the war stretches beyond four months. It is all very well to clip some camel traders in Egypt, it is another matter to fight a prolonged war against Cossacks in winter in snow.'

Consequent to the Women-billeting Wednesday, Jack Robinson's Wednesday evening suppers were not nearly as well attended as they had been previously. Some of the men found diversions about their quarters that proved of greater interest and reward than the company of their fellows. That being said, there came a certain Wednesday evening that saw a few of the soldiers with whom we are familiar and a chapter of the volume of boffins whom we have met, all gathered and assembled and about at Jack Robinson's. Their conversation had ranged widely, both in terms of content and in character; they had argued, fought, roared and laughed. Bargains had been struck and bets had been made and legs had been borrowed. There came a point at which Governor Rantallion reflected upon the weather.

'... against the Cossacks in winter in snow.'

'Did a fellow notice the undistilled energy that was a-rampant last night? Anyone? I recall that when I called upon you Thomas—midnight had passed—that it was a strange and wonderful evening.'

These Wednesday evenings at Jack Robinson's had developed certain conventions and routines over the last six or five months and one of them was that when the Governor made an obtuse and irrelevant contribution to the conversation then it was beholden upon the conversation to change tack and shift with him until he could be talked down. He added,

'Did you ever witness the wind so wild, the air so stirred, and one's blood so restless?'

'Yes, it was quite a night.' Said the Colony Botanist.

'Outrageous weather, it claimed my hat.' Said the Cartographer and the Second to the Quarter-Master contributed,

'An evening of wild distemper I say, and Napoleon be damned.'

The Governor stared sternly at the Colony Astronomer and was riled by that fellow's silence.

'What about you, Grand Night-Watchman? I would have thought you'd have had something proud and pompous to say about the weather, or were you too busy drawing pictures of my tossel?'

Since his disgrace the Colony Astronomer had often found himself baited and verbally belted and bullied in this manner; he was a quick thinker and reasonably adept at making good use of his thoughts and he fast discovered that the possible best stratagem was abject and servile capitulation.

'No, I didn't see anything. It was exactly as you have described it.' He said, and the sad silence that followed his blunt and brusque observation was fast filled by the Fleet Navigator, a fellow of whom we have heard naught to this point and who consequently requires some introduction.

As this novel has heaved into being and then lumbered into motion, as the words have tumbled down and settled into an approximation of sense and as I have raced backwards and forwards preparing them for your arrival, the confusing affairs of the Colony Astronomer's life have rendered him quite a different person to the gentleman I had at one time envisaged. He has changed, changed beyond my expectation, come up a completely different fellow to the one I had initially reared. I'm sure his mother feels likewise.

He was left like a chicken to baste and—freed up for other tasks—I have so worked the onions and so worked the seasoning and so worked the sauce that I soon discovered I required a duck. A duck with a good knowledge of the stars. Thank the heavens then, for the Colony Navigator. How fortuitous for everyone involved in this affair that John Drake the Colony Navigator had been awake and about on the evening prior, was present at Jack Robinson's soiree, and how fortunate that he was happy to discuss with the Governor the affairs of the preceding evening.

'I noted the disharmony of the night.' Declared the Colony Navigator. 'I was out, Sir, also about and spent the night awake—we are in a fine spot to trace the passage of Venus across these Heavens, Sir, it is a valuable location from which to map its course though I admit I do wish we were in Tahiti.'

'Tahiti!!' Echoed Beamish.

'Yes, the view from there is purported to be magnificent.'

'So you noted the weather then?' Inquired the Governor.

'Tahiti.' Repeated Young Corporal Beamish, again in apparent agreement with the Navigator but nodding his head in a happy pantomime of smug knowingness, cheekily hinting that he knew of things on a whole new level. 'Yeah, I've heard the view's pretty magnificent there too.' He said.

'It is the finest vantage we have on this earth from which to view the heavens, it is as if someone has opened a window to the cosmos.'

'Did you notice how much the wind was blowing?' Asked Governor Rantallion.

'Reckon I wouldn't mind being in Tahiti at the moment.' Said Captain Bridewell getting the whiff of a joke in the making and eager to lend it legs. Happily joining in on the riff that Beamish had got started and bumping it along to a whole new level. 'I reckon I'd have a go at a few of the old Passages of Venus myself.' His remark was greeted with delight by the non-commissioned men; they welcomed it with nudge and wink approval.

'From there the view would have been like ice shards, it would startle the eyes.' Resumed the Colony Navigator and Young Beamish offered,

'I hear there's a bit more than that to startle the eyes.' Happily and without any pretence that he had naught but lewd intent.

'Though I understand it is cloudy there, perhaps I enjoy good fortune.'

'It's not cloudy here, more windy of late.' Said the Governor.

'I had a mate back in Norfolk who had been to Tahiti and he said the girls there...' Said Young Beamish, as he wildly played every card he had. Either the conversation ran upon the lines he had been prompting or it stayed with the Navigator's vain ramblings, he had no other tricks at his disposal. It was between Beamish and the Navigator. The Governor had sadly folded. But on *Jack Robinson's Card Night* on the Wednesday of *The Week after the Billeting of the Women* the Colony Navigator had about himself the figurative equivalent of a trump card. He pulled rank.

'Excuse me, Young Beamish, but you rudely interrupt me time and time again with your tired and lewd musings and I must order you to desist. I am the proud owner I will tell you, of a good telescope, though a primary lens has been scratched by the clawed foot of one of these prevalent and pernicious land fowl.'

'Kurrapuuks.' Said Doctor Wilmot.

'Yes, indeed. Kurrapuuks.'

'If you eat them you go mad, mad and unholy mad.'

'Yes indeed, Doctor Wilmot, you have advised us of this fact a number of times. The scratch this kurrapuuk hen has caused is a horror, it contorts the angle of the view about 8.3 degrees, and it made off with my chicken sandwiches.'

'8.3 degrees?' Exclaimed the Colony Botanist and he gently dabbed his sweating brow whilst Young Beamish added,

'In coconut milk 'tis said they douche their sweet cunnies.'

'Have that man flogged.' Screamed Governor Rantallion. 'You were warned once you imp. I will not have you presume to merrily parade your lasciviousness.'

But somebody played another card. It was Captain Bridewell of all people. And it was the ten of the current trump suite.

'Governor Rantallion, I will not stand him flogged. You can butcher a man's brain, you can butcher his limping eye and the aspect of his step, but it is another thing again to butcher his body.' Said Captain Bridewell, immediately rising from his chair and readily fingering his sword and leaving the poor chair distraught at his feet in a state of dire disharmony.

'I think my friend here has a point.' Offered Jack Robinson. 'Though I cannot make sense of the butchery he describes. You cannot flog a man for voicing a thought. 'Tis not a just commission.' Said Jack Robinson and he bowered graciously to the Governor who stood surely to his left.

'I beg your pardon.' Said Governor Rantallion.

'You enjoy wonderful powers over this land, Dear Governor.' Said Jack Robinson wistfully. 'It is the case that they have not been matched since the time of the Emperors of Great Rome, to flog a man for bringing to the attention of company the will of his loins is not one of them. It is this man's inalienable right...'

'And I am quite sure you are wrong, Sir. This is Jacobite heresy and you are a fat villain. I must be able to flog a man for this sort of clarion call to depravity—I'm sure I have read of this. Captain Naskin, what do you know of this issue?'

'About the hen that took the chicken from the drake? Why I think it is a cock-up.'

'I beg your pardon.'

'And why was I not told?' Asked the Second to the Quarter-Master.

'Little of the Astronomer's lens, a little of the women of Tahiti.' Continued Captain Naskin.

'I beg your pardon immediately, Sir.'

'They are fine and hearty women, Sir, Young Beamish is correct in speculating with their ample promise, though his timing is perhaps ill-considered.'

'I warn you, Captain Naskin, if you persist in being deliberately obtuse...'

'No, nothing of the Navigator's lens, though I wonder that he did not note that on this Tuesday evening you both discuss it was as windy a night as I have ever seen.'

'Yes it was an almighty windy night last night. Yes Hurrah.'

'It blew the dull turf dumbly through the branches.'

'It was the better of many a proud tree.'

'I saw one cow who had found itself in such a situation that it must fast learn itself the ways of the koala bear.'

'Come, that's Capital.'

'And did you not note, Mr Navigator, that the moon on that night was in fact a full moon.'

'But by my leave, Captain Naskin.' Said Governor Rantallion. 'What on earth do you...?'

'Not on earth, Sir. Did not either of you gentlemen note the character of the moon?'

'It brought light to the branches and revealed my path certainly.'

'But it was a full moon.'

'The moon was a full moon?'

'No other thing could have been.' Said Captain Naskin and the Colony Astronomer said,

'Yes, I'll vouch for that.' And Captain Naskin added,

'Of course the wind was wild, of course the air was stirred and of course your blood was restless.'

'Was it anything like Monday Night?' asked the Colony Botanist and Captain Naskin continued,

'Distilled energy? Why what you felt was the earth unabounded. It is the night when every sea and every wave and branch and spirit of our world is unshackled and a-dancing. They are wicked nights, Sir, wild and wonderful. They can easily claim a fellow's hat, they can claim one's soul.'

And Captain Bridewell added,

'I know what you're finding wild and wonderful chum.'

'Last night, Sir.'

'You're talking like a fool spouting all this gypsy talk. You're snatch-struck and singing whatever you've been taught by your Spanish whore.'

'Goodness enough, Sir.'

'This is all gypsy talk, eh? Something he's learnt from his Spanish lady friend.'

'Your manners, Sir, I do declare.' Said the Colony Astronomer but Captain Bridewell persisted tangentially,

'You'll have us all worshipping goats soon, Naskin. Is that what your gypsy whore has been telling you?'

'I do not worship goats, Captain Bridewell, and it will not do you well to speak again of the Spanish Girl that way.'

'Do you worship goats eh, Naskin? Captain Naskin?' Asked Captain Bridewell again. He was in no way interested in the answer, merely delighted by the hearty nods and cheery support he received from the uniformed men each time he posed the question.

'It suffices me that I must daily salute one.' Replied Captain Naskin.

'Enough, Captain Naskin!' Said Governor Rantallion.

'An ill-considered reply, Sir, I thought its meaning would elude you, I apologise.'

''Tis all the same to those gypsy whores.'

'Captain Bridewell, you may have missed my first and second warnings and I allow that your last statement may not be intended to imply my current housekeeper. Sir, I entreat you not make another comment that I could take to speak ill of the Spanish Girl. William?'

'Ca-Captain Naskin?' Stammered William Casey the Colony Astronomer whose mind and thoughts had strayed from his fellow's conversation and who was giving address to memories of something he fast forgot.

'You're an astronomer. Tell these people what they need to know.'

'I beg your pardon, Captain Naskin.'

'About the moon.'

'Well...about the moon? Essentially...well it's like a cycle wherein the moon is shortly. I really don't know Captain Naskin. What is it you would have me say?'

'Just...just that it's logical that when two lunar bodies of the size of the earth and the moon...'

'Yes?'

'... Are at their closest point within their wild orbits that they pull and seize upon each other...'

'Yes they do. Of course they do. Understand that we live on what is technically a dual planet. If we saw our planet in a far away galaxy why we'd think it a mere star.'

'... The waves are stirred, why there's a tempest in the branches...'

'Our planet is primarily two profoundly malleable elements; liquid and gas, water and air.'

'The tides draw back with alarming haste, they build greater ferocity with each succeeding wave and crash violently upon the shore.'

'You can feel something stirring in the weather, in the wind, a passion in the night.'

The Colony Astronomer now fully understood what type of input was required of him by Captain Naskin, and he merrily warmed to the theme.

'Why in truth we can only in wonderment speculate as to what must be happening upon the moon but we fear great mountains must send thriving metropolises tumbling into the oceans, great canals must over reach and breach the walls and dykes and flood the villages and hamlets, that tidal waves engulf the valleys and drown the plains and show the pyramids an idle folly.'

'We do not dispose of our dead. They are still here amongst us. We do not cast their spirits from our realm. They are walking this day our every companions.'

'They feed our earth, they dance in our winds.'

'And when the earth and moon are at their closest junction, when they balloon inwards and outwards and the skies are sorely stretched there is cast open to the universe a window...'

'Explain that it is an open window.'

'...An open window and all the trapped spirits show their wild hearts and clamber to it. They try to escape.'

'Now that's definitely gypsy talk.' Said Fat Old Jack Robinson and he was fast disputed by Captain Naskin.

'It's plain old full-moon talk. We had these things in Europe. Did you gentleman have to travel half way across the globe to not note one?'

'It's all the talk your Spanish whore's been saying...'

'Right, you had enough warnings, chum. You're nicked.' Said Captain Naskin and he seized the sturdy, hewn table that had been so integral to their evenings' entertainments, that had borne their dinner and now was laden with the empty bowls and bare plates, the table that they had all so frequently left and forgot their empty glasses and bottles upon, that now played host to the many maps and books and charts that had been called upon and exhibited and consulted during the evening and which now lay discarded upon the sturdy hewn table, the table which Captain Naskin seized and heaved up and jolted around and, kicking the debris from his feet, bore before him across the room and pummelled against the startled figure of Captain Bridewell, who fast found himself squashed up against the wall.

Did Captain Naskin's actions startle everyone else in that room? They certainly startled everyone else in that room. Whom did they startle most of all? They most startled Captain Bridewell.

Poor Captain Bridewell was bewildered to somehow discover himself squashed up to the wall by some kind of door: 'Some kind of door it was a door and there was no door here—it's not a door, it's a door, it's a table, Good God.' He thought and behind it he heard someone whispering.

'It's only because you're an officer.' Said Captain Naskin. 'That I don't pull this handkerchief back and beat you into the floor like you were a seven-year-old cripple girl. It is because you are an officer that I shall do this.'

And he commenced hurling his full weight repeatedly against the table, the table and Poor Captain Bridewell behind it, the table and Poor Captain Bridewell between it and the wall.

Chapter 20   Poor Captain Bridewell

Captain Bridewell was a strong man, and he was a very sure man who had, in his days, seen a lot of this world. He had lived an interesting and a varied life, he could tell you a lot of stories about a number of places, a number of stories about this world and many of those tales he told in the arduous wrinkles and scars and creases of his face.

He had the defiant jaw of a twenty-year-old; it was confident and proud to stake its claim. He had the serious brow of a thirty-year-old, it had weathered enough storms and tempests during those succeeding ten years to know that nothing should still surprise. He had the wrinkles of a fifty-year-old, gentle wisps and gullies and crevices etched around his eyes that crinkled in wry amusement every time a younger man presumed to tell him a thing. He had the full hair of a man of twenty-four and the endearing dimples of an eight-year-old boy and all of these features were wildly out of place on the face of a man aged seventy-two. The brow, the dimples, the cleft, the crow's feet, the chin all created a wild discord about the man's face such that it was nearly impossible to reckon the fellow's intent. He was an immensely confusing person to look at.

It was all there to be seen in his eyes. These at least were the eyes of a seventy-two-year-old. It was there you could see his soul, it was appealing to be relieved of its burden. There were about twenty-seven different and wildly disparate years exploding off elsewhere on Captain Bridewell's face, all contradicting each other whilst clambering for attention; there were seventy-two years welling up in his eyes and begging to be relieved, to be free of their task.

His sad weepy eyes wallowed in the pools of a life lived too long, they entreated that they be forever rid of this mad burden, they unequivocally declared that this man had had enough, that he wished to retire, nay, expire, the man wanted out. But the fellow was clad in the fresh and proud uniform of a new recruit. He wore the hair of a man fifty years his junior, he set himself the most arduous tasks and brought unbridled energy to their execution. He would match the younger men drink for drink and mile for mile and he most often surpassed them.

His every action denied the forlorn entreaty of his tired old eyes, the man had an arsenal of affectations and ingenuities and entertainments to deny their sad petition.

Everyone knew Captain Bridewell was a tired old bucket; everyone knew he wished to be considered otherwise. They pampered his inane vanity.

If then for a moment, it may seem poor form of Captain Naskin to beat the sweet bejeebers out of this old man the age of seventy-two with a mighty oak table, please understand that to have done otherwise would have been wholly disrespectful.

CHAPTER 21   THE FALL OF CAPTAIN BRIDEWELL

The wall that Captain Bridewell found himself squashed against was not a great sturdy thing, it was not a grand and mighty bluestone affair such as one might encounter in Europe. It was made of flaky grey branches smothered in dust. It was a frame of bracken coated in daub to seal the spaces. These branches fast shed their water, they contained no sap, they were soon dry and brittle, the clay of this land was powdery and weak, it was not resistant to a firmly applied finger or thumb, it was no match for the rain. It was bare stockade against the cold chill wind and ice damp that settled in this valley. The snakes soon slithered through its gaps, the bush rodents soon nibbled through the bind. It was certainly not able to withstand the onslaught of two grown men and a big wooden table. It soon gave way and crumbled in a cloud of powder to the ground, with a few twigs leaping free and flying away in the wild wide wind.

Captain Bridewell fell through the cool air and then landed in the mud that featured in this particular part of Jack Robinson's Garden, the sty where he quartered his pigs. When he landed in that pool of mud he felt its cool and gentle soft hand cushion his body and surround his body and enclose his body and soothe every injury about his body and for a split-second each pin-prick of pain and anguish flew from his body but it was only for a split-second because then the table and Captain Naskin landed upon him. They forced the breath from his lungs and a number of teeth from his gums.

He felt the table drawn back but he was fast sinking into the mud and was ready to see if the cool mud could cure his pain from the *inside*. He sucked in the mud and let it slowly melt down his oesophagus. He let mud cool the burning in his eyeballs, the pain in his belly. But, oh, what, soon some wretched fingers propped his chin up, some wretched fingers dug the mud from his mouth.

Doctor Wilmot had quickly leapt down from the suddenly wall-less room and he wrenched Poor Bridewell from the clingy mud and sat behind him and dug the muck from his throat and rested Bridewell's head back against his chest. He leant his ear close over the man's mouth and, when confident that his breath had resumed a reliable pace he dug and wrenched Bridewell's arm from the mud, folded the putty fingers in upon themselves and shook the fellow's muscle-less fist angrily at Captain Naskin.

'Oh Jesus, Captain Naskin, you haven't made a friend here. I can barely hold him back.'

'We've had our disagreement, I'm willing to let the issue rest.'

'I'd suggest that if you were in this gentleman's position you might carry a grudge.'

'There shouldn't be a need for a grudge if he'd just note that I don't like him speaking ill of other people, Tahitians or Spaniards or Eskimos for that.'

'And perhaps not Spaniards in particular?'

'Doctor Wilmot, is there not enough in Captain Bridewell's condition to indicate the reward for that line of inquiry?'

'Quite right.' Concurred Doctor Wilmot. He addressed his next comment to all those in his company, the many men who stood about the pond. 'This man will need stitches to his brow. Immediately I will staunch that cut with a bandage and attend to it later. I must promptly apply lead powder to that wound there and return a few of those ribs to their preferred domicile, however I am completely at a loss in these affairs without my medicine bag. Could someone please fetch it from my quarters?'

Young Corporal Robertson, who had been observing affairs with considerable interest, at times bewildered and amazed, and at times concerned at these constant speculations about his fiancée's chastity, suddenly discovered himself being pointed at and shouted at and the words were a great confusion. Young Corporal Robertson, who had spent the whole night discreetly tending the shadows, who had not offered a word and yet had not missed one, was suddenly being barked at and pointed to and yelled at and told to disappear.

He was about to start crying when he suddenly discerned that he was being requested to race on over to the Doctor's house and pick up a bag and he bounded off immediately.

He was prompt to the Doctor's cabin and swift through the door and quick to take the Doctor's bag from where it sat upon the bare table and fast to fasten its fastener and when he returned to Jack Robinson's tri-walled house he gave the bag to the Governor who passed it to Captain Naskin who sat beside Doctor Wilmot and Captain Bridewell in the mud. Doctor Wilmot took it from him and unsnipped its shiny brass clasp.

It had eggs in it. They were beautiful eggs, beautiful and perfect eggs the size of a woman's fist, dear, strong and delicate eggs—pale brown, tan and chestnut, vaguely calimanco and speckled, busy and dustily spotted and freckled like the Convict Girl Becky's shoulders, like her shoulders and her arms and her bust, freckled like her dear sweet bosom and sure the size of her fist. Beautiful eggs set carefully and packaged tenderly on the straw and the leaves and the cloth—they were eggs, lovely eggs, wonderful eggs, as fine as any egg of Fabergé, but they were eggs nonetheless.

'Oh, that's right.' Said Doctor Wilmot. 'I left my instruments out at kurrapuuk Valley.' He said and held his breath for a while and then he added, 'I guess...' and then he finally breathed at that exact same moment that Captain Bridewell *finally* breathed.

Chapter 22   The Oration of Governor Rantallion

'I don't know which one of you to blame for this untimely death.' Said Governor Rantallion standing at the edge of the wall-less room to the men assembled pieta-like in the stinking piggywallow before him. 'It is perhaps the case that you are all equally responsible though perhaps Mr Bridewell is the most blameworthy. You were rudely provoked, Captain Naskin, and retaliated in kind, and whilst your response was markedly and perhaps excessively brutal this should surely have been anticipated by Captain Bridewell. John Wilmot, it is not fitting that you carry eggs in your medical bag where there should be instruments. You are a doctor, not a goose maid.'

'The bags were open.' Said Doctor Wilmot. 'There were plenty of sacks, there were other implements about the room if the soldier had have used his good sense...'

'This is the latest in a string of incidents. I have repeatedly been called upon to do your duties. Captain Naskin recently had to take to needle and potion...'

'I cannot be expected to anticipate every injury each malingering convict can contrive they...'

'I am of a mind to have you shot young fellow, do not interrupt me a third time. We all must attend a funeral tomorrow, that may or may not be due to your negligence. I may schedule another for Friday. As for you, Poor Dead Captain Bridewell... your many years lived show that you met most of the challenges a life can throw at a person and proved their master. I hope you enjoy such good fortune in the afterlife. We shall pray that you do not there encounter Captain Naskin. All of Captain Bridewell's belongings are to be taken to the Quarter-Master's Store, they can be requisitioned off—perhaps by auction—with the exception of his chess set, his leather bound and silver capped flask, his bed head and shaving kit which are to be impounded at my quarters.'

Governor Rantallion strode out the doorway and commanded in two convicts who had been passing by, with the intention that they might take Captain Bridewell to the Grave Master's

Infirmary where a coffin could be prepared. He wiped his hands upon his vest and continued,

'This man brought his death upon himself. Doctor Wilmot, it was you who failed to save him, I will decide what should result. Captain Naskin, I do not hold that you meant to kill him.'

And Convict Snivey sniffled and then he mumbled more to himself than anyone, 'Surprised Naskin'd have a care for anyone, what with that Spanish witch sucking every pint of seed out of his horrid root.' And he spat contemptuously upon the ground.

A number of things can be said about that last comment of Convict Snivey's. I shall restrict myself to three—firstly, that it was ill-considered; secondly, that it was mightily ill-timed; and thirdly, Oh Lord, it bore great ill for Snivey.

Chapter 23   The Pernicious Arab Convict

Later that evening, when at last Doctor Wilmot wearily and ruefully returned to his cabin, his considerable woes and concerns were immediately multiplied when he detected the Arab Convict standing deferentially by his small gate. The Arab Convict was reckoned and renowned about that colony as an expert watcher and a prime look-out. Why it was that misdemeanour—standing guard whilst his fellow lags stealthily did the nicking—that had indeed recommended him for transportation. Nobody was ever pleased to see him lurking by their door. It was a nefarious art for which the Pestiferous Arab was eminently well-suited, and it gave good purpose to three of the fellow's distinct and defining characteristics.

'Good evening.' Bellowed the Pestilential Turk. 'This is a good wind, a gentle wind is it not?'

Firstly, he was by disposition an expansive and compelling speaker, he enjoyed and eagerly sought conversation, he was difficult to evade and escape, he talked because he wished conversation and having secured it he would rarely brook interruption, annulment, excuses or attempts at extrication.

Concurrently, he spoke English as a second language (as a third in fact) and consequently he often found himself unsure of his footing, he was given to long pauses as he silently reckoned up the word he required, always patient and ever deliberate, given to frequent delays wherein he sought verification for his selections.

'Why it is a...a breeze, yes? Do I speak fairly in calling it, my dear friend, a breeze?'

Valuable seconds would tick by.

'It was a gust and I must excuse myself...' Said Doctor Wilmot, worrying considerably about the safe repose of his possessions. Thirdly, the Arab Convict was seven feet tall in an era when the average fellow was ludicrously shorter than he is today and he pushed the Doctor forcibly upon the chest and the Doctor fell quickly and in a blunder of stray limbs to the dusty hard ground. The Arab Convict fell heavily down upon the Doctor and directed all his weight to his right knee, his right knee which he dug into the Doctor's throat, and he held his fist before the Doctor's eyes.

'There is nobody stealing from your house. I was out and about this evening, at walk but not with wicked intent, as were you yourself, Sir, and you have simply met me here.'

'Gyyah.' Said the Colony Doctor and the Arab Convict lifted his knee from Doctor Wilmot's Adam's apple pancake. He shook his fist before the Doctor and then brought it in close to the Doctor's face, but a quarter inch from his nose.

'Why do you threaten me?'

'I am neither churlish nor wish you harm but have made my way here, Sir, to knock on your door, Sir, to bid you consider the condition of my knuckles. I am not a man well used to flaky and scabrous knuckles, Sir, of all my many years they have been so for only these past three days.'

'I have a lotion that'll fix that.' Said Young Doctor Wilmot. 'I'm sorry you feel the need to attack me to command my attention and shall rectify that matter.' Or words to that effect. 'Will you please, Sir, get off me. Come sit on my porch whilst I find the right bottle.'

The Arab Convict sat down by the Doctor's door and watched as the medic searched amongst his many bottles and vials and vessels and glass pots. He noticed a short jar away from the Doctor's general clutter of glassware, a small brown squat jar of potion that sat on the crate by the Doctor's bed. He pointed to the jar.

'Is that it on your bedside crate?'

'No. No, that's not it.' Said Young Doctor Wilmot. 'Now that, my friend, is a rather particular substance, an accomplished concoction of equal parts lotion and oil and water that I have contrived for my own self-pleasuring. No, this one here is the one we want. Now, let's look at those knuckles.'

And the Arab Convict rested his hands upon his knees and considered the Doctor's balding cranium as the fellow applied the stinging lotion to his corrupt and poisonous joints. He turned up his eyes towards a tree and saw two birds fighting. One of them overcame the other and pecked at its neck until it separated the head from the body.

'I'll tell you a story about two birds that this fellow saw fighting.' Said the mighty Arab Convict and the Doctor said, 'Mhm.'

CHAPTER 24   THE STORY OF QAMAR AL-ZAMAN

'Qamar al-Zaman is the gentleman's name and he is sitting afraid and totally aghast at the sheer desolation of his life, he's got himself a stack of problems, and he's just tripped over in the orchard where he weeps. Soon he looks up to a tree.

He turned up his eyes towards a tree and saw two birds fighting. One of them overcame the other and pecked at its neck until it separated the head from the body. Then it flew away with the head while the other bird fell dead to the ground in front of Qamar al-Zaman. Soon two big birds swooped down, and one stood at the neck of the dead bird and the other at its tail and, folding their wings, stretched their necks towards it and wept. When Qamar al-Zaman saw the birds weeping for their companion, he wept at his separation from his wife. The birds dug a hole, in which they buried the dead bird, and then they flew up in the sky. After a while, they returned, bringing with them the bird that had killed the other. They alighted with it on the grave of the slaughtered bird and, crouching on it, killed it. Then they cut open its belly, tore out its entrails, and spilled its blood on the grave of the slaughtered bird. Then they strewed its flesh, tore its skin and, pulling out all its innards, scattered them in different places.

'All this happened while Qamar al-Zaman watched in amazement.'

'What do you mean, Sir?' Asked Young Doctor Wilmot as he concluded daubing the Arab's knuckles with the foul-smelling lotion. He screwed the lid back upon the jar and passed it to the Arab Convict. 'Reapply this every night and don't pick at the scabs.'

'I merely tell you a story from the Arabian Nights.'

'It is a fine story. Now if any of those birds had tried eating a kurrapuuk they would have gone mad, mad, unholy mad.'

'It is a tale told by our parents to our children.'

'What does it mean?'

'I do not know the tale, Sir.'

'Does it mean that there are lessons we can learn from the ways of the birds?'

'Either that, or from the ways of the Arab.'

Chapter 25   Doc Wilmot

I don't know which way to jump with Young Doctor Wilmot. I don't know whether to condemn him for his negligence or pity him for his haplessness. I don't know whether to draw him a pompous buffoon or sketch him a belaboured soul. I don't know whether to demonify him for his self-obsession that led to so much woe, or admire his sheer resilience and refusal to be cowed by the more immediate demon that was his struggle with madness. I certainly reckon it's a bit rough that he got eaten. That they cut open his belly, tore out his entrails, and spilled his blood upon the ground. That they strewed his flesh, tore his skin and, pulling out all his innards, scattered them in different places. All a bit rich. Whatever you decide about Doctor Wilmot, you can't deny he had pluck.

Chapter 26

'I'll shoot him.' Said Governor Rantallion to the Colony Astronomer who had fast left the scene of Captain Bridewell's death, nervous that he might somehow find himself implicated in the affair, and had to his distress found himself walking the same path as the Governor. He didn't like Governor Rantallion, he didn't like the fact that they were walking alongside each other, and yet he now found himself speeding his stride to keep pace. He snuck quick glances up at Governor Rantallion and assessed his mien.

'I was of a mind to shoot you for your wretched filthy pictures, I feel similarly prompted to damn this man for his more ruinous mischief.'

'Yes, shoot him.' Said the Colony Astronomer. 'Align the muskets and powder his head.'

'Tomorrow at dawn.'

'I'll with distinction add my bullet to his woes.'

'Why, if he can't control his temper well then I'll damn well still it.'

'Who?'

'Why Captain Naskin.'

'No, don't shoot Captain Naskin.'

'Well, who should I shoot?'

'Shoot the Doctor my fickle Lord. If a man is to be shot for this affair why it must be the Doctor. If not Sergeant Salt than surely the Doctor. His vanity places us all at peril, his negligence may yet damn us.'

'He is of no mind to perform his duties.'

'Barely a doctor at all.'

'Captain Bridewell but for the Doctor's neglect...'

'He is a danger to us.'

And the two gentlemen continued their passage emboldened by the brilliant simplicity of their audacious resolution, fortified by the eminent obviousness of the solution, and proud of their precise powers of deduction until the Colony Astronomer stumbled upon a tree root that the moonlight had not seen fit to reveal and which sent him toppling off to the left where he tripped into a bush and then scrambled down a scree and then painfully crinked his ankle as he fell wildly over a log.

'Be damned but we need a doctor.' He said as he frantically rubbed each pain upon pain. 'We just need a doctor who's around.'

'Yes, a doctor who is available at all times and in all situations.' Agreed the Governor and he sighed ruefully as he pondered the unimpounded impossibility of his task and the Colony Astronomer said,

'You need to kill all the birds.' And Governor Rantallion said, 'Damn.'

Chapter 27

'You are poorly suited for a man who has been playing cards with friends.' Said the Spanish Girl and Captain Naskin replied,

'Oh, I'm a mess.'

'Are you often so filthy?'

'I had a discussion with another gentleman in the pool where Robinson's pigs cool themselves.'

'You finished up battling in a pig pond?'

'Aye.'

'Dammed Hogwash.'

'That be the place.'

'Boorish and boarish.' Said the Spanish Girl to which Captain Naskin replied,

'You have a proud wit tonight ma'am and 'tis a fair observation.'

'I shudder at your appearance.'

'A dispute arose.'

'But you were playing cards, you boisterous fellow.'

'We discussed other matters.'

'Just have a look at yourself.'

'Yeah, I'm filthy.' Said Captain Naskin and he retreated outside to remove his stinking boots and the Spanish Girl resumed the customary position that had been hers for the past five hours as she had sat and listened to the night—her chin set upon her palms, her elbows set upon the surface of the table, the surface of the table beset with a great waiting mess of playing cards which the Spanish Girl now noted, she now noted before her a great number of playing cards scattered at will and wildly and she heard the boot of the mad and murderous man fall heavily upon the wooden step outside.

"Tis said you had the old snuff-cove Albert Snivey flogged to death.'

'How have you heard of that?' Asked Captain Naskin, yelling over his shoulder to the open door behind him whilst struggling with his second boot.

'What?'

'How have you heard of that?' Repeated Captain Naskin and he sat for a moment and stared down at his empty boots and watched then a dear little bronze tree frog with thin rims of gold around its pale blue and red eyes and fine ruby mottled green skin that, having got itself into the middle of Captain Naskin's path, had lost its bearings and didn't know whether to finish his journey this way or that.

'This is a very small town, Sir. We all heard his cries.'

'It wasn't a good sound.' Said Captain Naskin and he staggered tiredly back into the room and—with a hint of merry pantomime to the gesture—waved a weary 'goodbye' to his boots and then he looked at the Spanish Girl, noted her injury from the assault some weeks prior, and he said,

'Are you still rinsing your bloody stitches with vinegar?' As he sat down beside her at the table.

'Yes.'

'Every evening?'

'Yes.'

'I have asked you not to. Do you know...?'

'Yes I do.'

'And the chance of...'

'I have noted it.'

'So the...'

'You have told me, surely... I know not. Four dozen times?'

'Then why do you persist?'

'It is my people's remedy.' Said the Spanish Girl and she brought her hands down roughly upon the table and her fingernails made a tremendous clatter upon the surface and she immediately evacuated her calamitous hands to the snug safety of her lap.

'But the vinegar of this land is not pure enough for that purpose—over and above that it is nonsense to apply a sour astringent to any wound so deep—with the vinegar of this land it is particularly unwise. The risk of infection...'

'It is what our mothers and their mothers have done for centuries, Sir.'

'But they were in Europe for God's sake, woman.' Said Captain Naskin and he grabbed the heavy four-litre stoneware and cane demijohn of vinegar from the slate cooking bench and heaved it out the door and cast it roughly out into the night. Squish. 'Their vinegar was from the pure hills of Greece, it was from the lush plains of Italy. The vinegar in this land is potato sweat.'

'And still I will mind my mother before you, Sir. You spoke of the convict Snivey.'

'I spoke of who?'

'Of Albert Snivey. You have killed him?'

'Not directly.'

'But you had him killed? You slayed him?'

'So that's what this is all about?'

'Old Bert Snivey is dead, is he? He is dead by your hand?'

'And that's why you're all out of sorts is it? He was a fellow lag and is that it and then?'

'He's dead because you whipped him?'

'Dead and all and so you think me a foul man?'

And the Spanish Girl answered,

'Albert Snivey was a wretched sack of rat paste. He has tramped so many of these women here about this colony that few among us don't know the smug tang of his issue, a number bear the damned child of his seed. There were few that mourned his dying screams, a great many cheered them. Will you answer me, Sir, was it you did the whipping?'

'He was assigned under the Governor and therefore the Navy and as we are arranged here, as a soldier...'

'That's a pity. Still, I think that I shall not play cards with you.'

'Madam?'

'I could not endure such havoc.'

'You can hardly infer...'

'To be rousled in a sty? To be flogged for... what crime was it? A brace of Diamonds? No Sir. I have seen your ire roused in our own games. Now I know its full measure I cannot dare to endanger myself.'

'Yet...'

'There will be...' But the Spanish Girl stopped mid-sentence, she held her breath and listened whilst Captain Naskin did likewise. They sat there still and alert, neither one passed nor drew breath. They had both heard the sound upon the roof, the thud, the crash, and then the sound of the feet clambering down from the branches, heard the feet trace a slow and steady route across their roof, sat there in silence as the iron sheeted roof groaned and buckled under the weight of each steady step.

'Same damn possum.' Said Captain Naskin.

'Yes, you can hear the scratch of his claws.' Replied the Spanish Girl and she added, 'And still I shall not play cards.'

'Then we shall pass many a long and sorry evening.'

'If they are nights that I keep the skin upon my back, Sir, and keep from the pig pool, then I'll count my blessings. There will be no more cards.'

'Dice then?' Said Captain Naskin and the Spanish Girl replied, 'Can you play chess?'

Chapter 28

'Damn.' Said Governor Rantallion.

Governor Rantallion had had two years' training as an historian, he had for many years neglected the art but he hadn't forgot it. He knew that he now each day of his life wrote his own dear name upon a page of history, perhaps only in some poor and sorry footnote, but it was his name and it was his life and it would be his song, his. He knew the special disdain and mirth history reserved for the vain and preposterous. The askance and derisive humour with which follyful (sic.) King Canute is regarded for once bidding that the sea heed his rule, the bewildered glee and derisory hooting with which Caligula's exploits are marked in making war upon Poseidon and bidding his legions put their swords to the waves and taking the crabs and the walruses as hostages and prisoners of war and seizing the shells as booty. That and other stuff. History was full of derisible buffoons, lusty old King Harry and stuttering, stammering Claudius and vain old Nero and the disaster-wracked and disaster-prone rulers of France. Governor Rantallion had long hoped that his life would bear the marks and adventure of a Shakespearean drama, full of bold machinations, betrayal, jealousy and Byzantine intrigues, of mighty battles and stirring victories, of valour and honour and grand St Crispian's Day speeches. He had never hoped that it be one of the lesser comedies. He had hoped to be a Caesar not a Falstaff, a King and not a Belch and yet now here he was, he was here Grand

Governor Arthur Rantallion, obliged to declare war upon a brace of ducks. 'How...disagreeable.' Thought Governor Rantallion. 'I would I could wash my hands of this matter.' Thought Governor Rantallion and he took a moment to recognise the reference that had framed his thought, that had provided the hand-washing metaphor and then, on recognising it, immediately saw his solution. 'Yes, that's it.' He said, 'I'll get someone else to do it.'

'Wonderful Mr Casey, you've quite hit the nail on the head. Tomorrow at dawn we will arm you with four hundred convicts with thrashing sticks and rocks and have them compel to a point of common execution...'

'You wish me to emu march the kurrapuuks?'

'Indeed, sir.'

'But these are short little fellows with squat portly legs. They are no match to the mighty-legged emu.'

'It will take longer.'

'So it shall. But this is a preposterous duty. I am never the man for this task.'

'You are precisely the fellow.' Said Governor Rantallion, enjoying for a moment his companion's discomfort. 'The Doctor shall surely give protest so I'll send him out to John Dunnock Rock under the pretence of giving the man a constitutional.'

'I have had no contact with the convicts. They will not know whether to obey me or hang me.'

'And you shall have the Colony Fife Player and the Standard Bearer and the Regiment Drummer to accompany your efforts, to lend a rousing overture to this grand campaign and stir the convicts to greater endeavour.'

'What of the Colony Rat Catcher? He has made war against the vermin of the land, he will have learnt tricks and traps and stratagems that mark him the man for this commission.'

'Oh, very well.' Grumbled Governor Rantallion 'You've talked your way out of this one.' He said and then suddenly noted that they had reached that point where their journeys no longer shared a common route. 'I will send word to the Colony Rat Catcher at once.'

And he politely farewelled the Colony Astronomer and wished him good fortune to which the Colony Astronomer replied, 'I hope, Dear Governor, you enjoy a fair repose.' And he bid that his dreams should be sweet.

Part IV

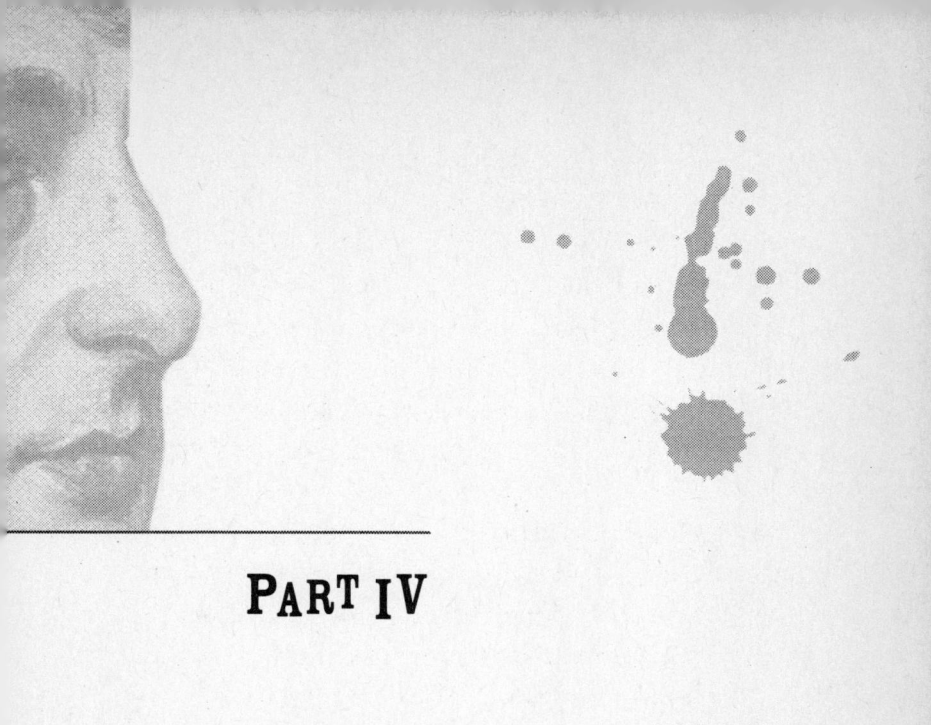

CHAPTER 29

Young Doctor Wilmot didn't feel this way or that about any day—though he'd certainly made a hash of yesterday—and he now found himself on a wretched boat sailing out to a wretched man on a wretched rock in the middle of the bay.

'So then you've all found a space for me?' Said Young Doctor Wilmot as he clambered awkwardly aboard the rowboat. 'Ahuh? I must check upon John Dunnock. The Governor said he must be well ripe by now.' Said Young Doctor Wilmot as the convicts wearily grumbled and shuffled about and found him room.

'Here. This'll do nicely. All Right.' Said Doctor Wilmot as he made himself comfortable upon one of the low-lying benches and settled his sack of tools upon his lap. 'If we must, we must. Let's get this over with.'

And the rowers began to row.

'This man has chicken pox.' Said Doctor Wilmot inspecting the rower to his left. 'Get him confined at once. Isolate him until I return. We need a rower without chicken pox.'

'Convict Collins.' Screamed Captain Herring. 'Collins, attend here immediately. Collins, this man is sick and cannot row the boat as commissioned. I call upon you to abruptly race up that hill and bid Bulltrunk hither that he may take the fellow's place.'

But instead Convict Collins abruptly fell to the ground and wept and cried and rubbed dust into his eyes to the surprise of not one of them. It was cruel of Captain Herring to have played this mean trick on Convict Collins, every person there knew it; it was also modestly amusing. Everyone enjoyed a big laugh except of course Convict Collins who enjoyed a big cry and then Convict Bulltrunk jogged down the slope of his own volition and took his place in the boat.

Chapter 30 Convict Collins

Amongst the ranks of prisoners Young Jack Collins, the eighteen-year-old burglar, was the only one out of the lot of them who actually wished to get selected for rowing duty.

They all hated rowing the boats 'cept Collins; he dearly desired it.

It was obvious to everyone: he wished it with all his heart. Craved it, willed it, coveted it and yearned, he was eager to be selected to row the boat. Young Jack Collins, the little burglar not yet twenty who—in an ironic twist—was so frequently having his person burgled by so many of the other male prisoners, had wished for months that on Wednesday mornings as they worked by the docks, he would be selected by Corporal Beamish to row John Dunnock's provisions out to John Dunnock on John Dunnock Rock. He made this desire obvious to everyone. There was no doubting it. *'I inkle that Young Collins wants to row out to John Dunnock Rock. Aye, 'tis the whisper.'*

On Wednesdays he would do not a scrap of work all morning, he'd barely snap a twig, but when Young Beamish came tripping and stumbing down Arthur Rantallion Scree at fifteen minutes past eleven, Collins would be working very hard indeed.

And he'd keep working very hard while Young Beamish explained to Captain Herring exactly the same thing that he explained to him every Wednesday morning. Then they'd both look about the men, chat and whisper and select eight. Collins would be about six feet away from them and he'd be working like the furies. He never got picked, Cockburn, Hook and Snivey with Nick the Buffer were the ones who got picked, Pillard One and Pillard the Lurker, Pitt the Fencer and Pollard the Hedger were the ones Beamish selected, Collins—never.

Collins was a superbly built fellow, wonderful muscle tone, he was sinewy and lean, the type who'd make a great sprinter, a reliable marathon runner, but a hopeless rower. He was never going to be selected to row that boat, Beamish picked the blokes who were made out of log.

Collins always made his disappointment at not being selected obvious to all. He was a slightly campy fellow, a bit of an *act-uh*, so when he dropped his shoulders mournfully and scowled and shook his head, when he cursed under his breath and shook his fist to the sun, it was obvious that to have not been selected to row the boat was a bitter disappointment. When he began cocking his head soulfully and putting the back of his hand to his brow, when he began moaning and gnashing upon the dust, Old Nulihan would compel the gratitude of all by informing him that everyone had got his point.

'Ne'er you mind son. Chance be you'll be rowin' that tub next week.'

It was a lie, a fairly obvious lie, but over the months it had proven to be the most reliable way of making Collins get back to an approximation of work.

But, a Wednesday came that was slightly out of whack. Everyone could sense it, everyone could feel it and everyone was sneaking glances at Jack Collins to see if the extreme tension might make his head explode. There came a Wednesday morning where suddenly everyone knew something was different, it wasn't so much a mood thing and it wasn't a mystical kind of thing, it wasn't the fact that the whole bush was suddenly eerily still or that there was a momentous portent in a sudden shift of the wind, it was that Nick the Buffer's leg was broke and Albert Snivey had been flogged to death by word of Captain Naskin. It would soon be revealed that Cockburn had chicken pox.

This morning, we'd be having a new line up.

They pointed out this convict over here and they assessed this one over there, they rued the injury of Nick the Buffer and they cursed the death of Snivey. They surveyed the ranks of working men before them and I tell you, Collins was going off. He was like a steam train, you've never seen a person work harder, an hour of it, and he could have built a pyramid.

Why Collins wanted to get out there, out there to John Dunnock Rock, out there to the crop of rock where the Young doctor was going to be stabbed to death with a knife in his neck within that very hour, was not as obvious. In fact, it was not known to a soul except Collins himself. And even he did not understand the strange progress of events that compelled his will, that made seeing John Dunnock his heart's desire. Even he didn't understand.

I'll be brief.

John Patrick Pulham (a.k.a. John Dunnock) was not an evil man, he was not a wicked man. If he is to be called a sinful man at least it was one of the honourable sins, it is the one where you thieve to feed your babies.

John Dunnock was a cobbler.

And he was a very fine cobbler.

He loved the craft and he was proud to be skilled at it. He was honoured to spend the hours studying it, and he matched those hours with time spent perfecting it. Had he spent a fraction of that time in the study of foreign affairs he might well have anticipated England's annexation of India, and foreseen the implications that would hold for the local boot industry. He did not. So when all those cheap shoes put together by those magnificently skilled slaves suddenly buried the whole of England, he had no plan. He had not devised the means by which he could survive it. Concurrently, he had a wife and fast two babies to feed and not a penny.

Fortunately for John Dunnock, he was well liked, he was widely respected, and when his troubles became known, two of the neighbourhood lads cut him in gently on a safe and easy job. John Dunnock stared temptation in the eye, and when all temptation required of him was that he stand on a street corner and keep a look-out, John Dunnock found himself tempted. For food enough to feed his babies for a month, he was prepared to keep an eye out while some poor local lads pilfered from some rich gentry; if Satan claimed his soul for it then that would just have to be the way it was going to have to be.

Sadly, whenever you hear these sorts of stories they all tend to have a common theme. An honest citizen takes that first small and safe step, they find themselves standing in a very slippery place indeed, a slippery place that inevitably leads to greater crimes and more daring misdemeanours, and then ultimately to their ruin. A sad and sure progress of cause and effect, of decline and fall, of temptation and descent that has been sufficiently documented elsewhere.

John's personal Oops-a-Daisy was that the 'departures' became more regular and more dangerous, that in these 'endeavours' he was promoted from watcher to intruder without his permission or consent, that 'enterprises' were being risked that promised a gain so mighty they would forfeit considered thought. That he had been swept into a dangerous and destructive whirlpool of deceit, criminality and decline.

When the job on Hobson's Chaff Bindery went haywire he ran, he ran with the rest and the best of them, he ran to the hills, and he hid out till it was safe for him to get home. When that didn't happen he joined in the attack upon the farm to get themselves food to live. He went with the band to Blackpool, he made a life with these blackguards that wandered the country and made danger in the night. He kept himself alive until he could go back home to his wife and his hearth and his dear little boys. It took an inexplicable period of time, but in John Dunnock's head and in John Dunnock's heart, these protracted wanderings that took him all around England and Ireland and to America for six years, were in fact a rather circuitous route back to Gloucester.

Understand that to find himself a convict—My God, a prisoner on a ship of prisoners, sailing away to New South Wales, the furtherest spit of England, in the middle of the fartherest Sea of the Earth, for the Term of his Natural Life—rather stymied his intentions.

It broke John Dunnock's heart. He was sailing, he was sailing away from his wife and baby forever, and he wasn't really clear on how he'd got here. He knew one boy had died, heard it from a traveller, happened when a barrel come off a cart onto his head. Squashed him flat. He never seen his other baby, was still in Lizzie's belly when he was forced away, and Lord knows he missed her too.

It makes complete sense then that he tried to smuggle a bit of them on board. That somewhere about that ship or upon his person he tried to transport with him the hope of them. This wasn't some illicit form of contraband that he sneaked onto that ship which needed a loose plank or a hidey hole to conceal it, some outlawed tools of his trade, or smuggled diamonds or coins, it was a vain wish and a poor hope and a hopeless, hopeful dream he carried in his heart which to be really effective, should be materialised in the form of a person, ideally, two people.

He knew he had a son, a son who would be eighteen, a son he had never seen. Concurrently, he was quite well disposed to Young Jack Collins the Burglar who he had heard was from the same town, who he could see was quite comely, who he knew spoke frequently of his mother and yet had no tales of his Da.

It was not hard for mad John Dunnock to convince himself that Young Collins was his son, and once that connection had been made, quite foreseeable that he would take umbrage at the frequency with which his son was being mishandled. He discreetly kept an eye on proceedings and observed every godless act and bloody violation of his very son, and when circumstances allowed him the opportunity to confront the primary abuser, he did so with a rock.

The rock John Dunnock picked up and then crushed into FitzHughes' head was not sufficient to kill the man, but it was sufficient to get John Dunnock shipped out to another, significantly larger rock in the middle of the bay.

None of this was understood by Collins. He knew a filthy and grubby old madman had been shipped to a rock in the middle of nowhere, and he had been told that he was somehow involved in the affair, that the madman was trying to defend his honour. He was keen to get into a boat and get out there and get a look at this mad fellow, see if getting a look at the old coot could somehow inform this circumstance with the touch of sense.

He was obsessed with the idea of getting out to that island. It was a bitter-sweet obsession; it gave him the will and reason to live in a hellsent landscape and a mad land that seemed to be constantly laughing at him, but it was an obsession that was constantly dashed, and that constant and unrelenting dashing was slowly driving him mad. He could obsess all he bloody well wanted, he was never, ever going to be selected for rowing duty, and for that, ultimately, he should consider himself blessed.

Had Young Jack Collins the Burglar been selected for rowing duty on the Wednesday morning when Nick the Buffer had him his leg troubles and after the death of Convict Snivey, I'm sure he would have got himself quite a surprise. He would have seen, perhaps not seen—it happened so quickly—but certainly have witnessed, certainly have been present, when a young doctor got himself stabbed in the neck by a filthy old man. He would have seen a sudden torrent of thick blood explode from that doctor's neck, seen his face go white with shock and horror, seen his head twitch back and in an instant become a skull, seen that skeleton drop, the dead limbs fall, seen more of that blood spurt from the gullet—tomato relish red—and spill down on the sun-cooked flesh like it was rich chutney.

Had Young Collins gone out to that island I am sure he would not have enjoyed it.

He was a convict, true, but this was not his kind of thing.

'Collins.' Screamed Captain Herring. 'Collins, attend here immediately. Collins, this man is sick and cannot row the boat as commissioned. I call upon you to abruptly race up that hill and bid Bulltrunk hither that he may take the fellow's place.'

Chapter 31   The Colony Rat Catcher

The Colony Rat Catcher looked about himself and looked at the great pile of dead birds and thought that he had about himself a job well done. He had initially barely understood the directives he had received from Governor Rantallion, but the more and more he looked at his surroundings the more and more he was able to convince himself that these situations at least met one or two of the demands. He reflected that he had somehow successfully achieved his mission without ever at any point being completely aware of it, it had all occurred as if by some kind of merry—*and at that moment he turned to the Regiment Drummer and the Colony Fife Player and bid that the former commence a quick impromptu drum roll please, a drum roll that should excite and rouse anticipation in the listener*—happenstance. It had all occurred as if by some kind of merry *happenstance*. He leant his right arm against a branch and discovered that it was cool *to the touch*. In the dew that had formed upon a handy leaf he snuck quick glances up at his reflection and assessed his mien. He wished that he was taking his breakfast.

His attentions to the branch suddenly disturbed a great shower of rainwater that fell upon him, and concurrently he dislodged a deep scab that sent stabs of pain throughout his person and then serendipitously he remembered his surroundings and he considered the great Kosciuszko of poultry he had enjoined his compatriots to amass and then, happenstantially, he remembered the existence of rats about this planet and considered the proximity of this mesa of fresh carcasses to the colony and could do nothing but conclude that such a pile of fresh and unattended meat could not help but attract rats. At which point he panicked. Attract rats to a place that he was meant to be keeping rat free. Oh No. Now he had to get rid of the dead birds, God damn it. He wondered if the dead kurrapuuks could just be pushed off the cliff, pushed off into the rough waves and into the raging ocean where they would fast be devoured by sharks. He looked over the edge of the rugged outcrop of rock and saw that there was a beach some sixty feet below, a beach with pristine and kindly undulating dunes that stretched for half a mile out to the gently lapping shallows. Kicking the chickens off the cliff would just lead to them splattering everywhere and then the convicts would have to troop off down to the beach and try to find each and every bit of each and every one of them and then trek them to the shoreline where the tide would fast return them. That would take hours. 'Time to call for help.' He thought but then he thought. 'No, actually.' He thought. 'I could just set fire to them. Burn them all up, that'll do the job.' 'Clever and novel approach.' He thought.

He then looked about and began searching for those items he would need to build this mighty bonfire—dry wood and branches in particular, great sturdy logs and sun-parched dead trunks, and he noted the generous quantity of dry twigs and starched bracken he had about him, the parched ferns and sticks and fronds that lay about a-plenty on this precarious peninsula of outcrop. 'Would kindling do?' Wondered the Colony Vermin Man as he considered the ample kindling that littered this vain reach of land, would kindling suffice to fuel this mighty bonfire he envisaged, this bonfire that would be so grand and so magnificent it would immediately compel the attention, awe and admiration of every person about that place and they would think it a fine thing indeed. 'Would kindling do?' Would it suffice to bring his small and wretched life to the dramatic attention of the people with whom he shared a home and would it leave them forever grateful that they had shared a home with him? Nup. He fast realised that kindling would not do it by half. He further considered his surroundings and regarded the great pile of dead birds, the mountain of drying carcasses, the hill of oily-feathered carrion and wondered whether that would suffice to fuel the great bonfire, would carrion suffice to fuel the grand spectacle he envisaged, would that compel their respect, could that compel their regard, could that ensure their good opinion, could carrion do for firewood?

Please.

Thought the Colony Rat Catcher and he found a match low and clad in the lint of his trouser pockets and he lit it against the flint he had discovered upon the handy and ingenious knife he had stolen from the drunk Swiss soldier. He cast the lit match upon the pile of oily dead birds and as they lit a sound erupted so profound and so resounding that no person there could have accurately described its nature and that I myself writing some two centuries later very much doubt I could barely approximate.

Chapter 32

Not one person there could have spoke the word that described the sound those birds made when they were exploded, less people amongst them could have envisaged the smell.

Had any one of them preconceived or anticipated the horrendous stink these poisonous carcasses would make when suddenly set alight they would have been wrong, wrong, wrong because when Doctor Wilmot had described the physical composition of these creatures he had told lies, lies, lies.

These were lovely plump birds, they were better than chicken, they were better than goose. You had not lived until you had eaten this bird and Doctor Wilmot knew it for a fact because a family of natives had once given him some and later explained its nature.

It was all like the best of every other poultry and honey and pepper all in one.

He was by now so taken with these birds that he forswore of ever eating a bit of one again—it was enough that he knew—he was certainly going to do everything within his power to make sure that none of those bloody wolves back in Old & New Bridgeford ever got their teeth around one.

He told everyone unceasingly about the poisonous meat and flesh of these birds, how their blood contained an oil that secreted into the flesh, how the local natives had told him that if you eat their flesh you went mad, stark mad, and how you ended your days naked in the dirt using a stick to dig your head off. You could not meet the man without him mentioning it. The meat of the kurrapuuk would make you go mad. He was right of course—ultimately the meat of the kurrapuuk did make a lot of people mad, whoa, the meat of those birds unleashed an ungodly torrent of dementia and horror amongst these hungry souls that knocked that there colony to the point of extinction—but he was right in a way that he could not have envisaged.

Chapter 33

As our age and era hurtles into the future one hears this and that about the speed of light and the speed of sound and how the former is faster than the latter, and how at the speed of one or the other this place here is thus far away, but you never hear that much about the speed of smell. From personal observation I've discovered that occasionally it is faster than my body moving away from a place of private misdemeanour but on other occasions it is slow and turgid and requires the urgent fanning of my arms to impel it up from its place of origin deep within the bedclothes. Perhaps it suffices for you to understand that on this occasion, out there in the bay of Old & New Bridgeford, when a thousand birds were slaughtered and ten starved men stood on a rock, the speed of sound was considerably faster than the speed of smell.

The speed of sound raced across that choppy bay and carried with it the unholy scream of a thousand birds being massacred, it was amazing that sound they found when they were forced to search their vocal chords and search their soul for a sound that could describe their anguish and describe the unutterable, the sound compelled one man mad and he struck another and he died for his troubles.

It was one hell of a hullabaloo.

It was nothing compared to the smell. It took the breeze about an extra five minutes to carry the smell of those cooking birds out to John Dunnock Rock. On the mainland the delicious smell had, by now, effected a bloody insurrection, the starving convicts were drove demented by the splendid aroma rising from the makeshift barbecue and had leapt upon the cooking birds and feasted upon their flesh. With weapons filched and weapons pilfered they made war with the soldiers who sought to suppress their bold sedition. All hell had broke loose.

When that smell hit John Dunnock Rock, nine boys who frequently thought themselves very hungry suddenly thought of nothing else. As if things weren't bad enough standing out there on that island with the body of the dead doctor cooking slowly and crackling crisply in the warm sun, they were about to become incredibly and irresistibly ravenous.

Cannibalism hey? I tell you, this story has it all. There are so many points at which these people's lives took the wrong turn that it can only stagger the modern reader. What sort of story were they writing of themselves? I survey their ranks and struggle to find an honourable person in their company and yet at each point a character fouls, another shows me a greater villainy. Had they no conception of themselves? Did they not realise that to eat the dead man to survive the night meant to wake the next morning as the type of person who had eaten another human being the day before? Did that sort of thing not bother them?

That two hundred years later gentle readers might read and observe that behaviour and hold it displays a want of character.

Probably not.

Obviously not.

I can't for a moment conceive of their behaviour but then again I've never been squeezed out of the anus of the land I called home. I've never been shat, spat and cast off to the dead bones of a poisonous carcass calling itself a land and told to make myself a home and scrape together an existence or, at the very least, ensure that the Union Jack can be seen by any ships that sail by. I guess in those circumstances I'd be a completely different person. All these years later I can perhaps utilise that heritage to explain some of my idiosyncrasies but I don't think I can really envisage it.

Nor could my Great-Great-Great-Great-Grandfather when he heard of it later.[4] It bewildered him. At the time he didn't even notice the rowboat when it returned from John Dunnock Rock—oh so much later than normal—he did not notice the soldier and prisoners move sheepishly and fearfully away from it as if anticipating a mighty whacking. He did not note the blood on their tunics. He had not been there when the Doctor

---

[4] Those of you who have just quickly referred to the cover of this book to confirm my family name as King and have returned to this page, scanned the text below, and found it contains the word at least two or three times and are now seething restlessly and grinding their teeth; those of you who have not noted a character called King thus far and are now daring me to show dastardly, bloody-minded gall and temerity by introducing this new character 'King' of whom we've heard not a whit thus far—this or that Prisoner King or Young Sergeant King or dear old Captain King beloved by his men—chill. Might I remind you that I am as much the child of my mother as that of my father, and that whilst I might not share her name I certainly share her lineage. That she could conceivably be descended from one of those who made their home in Old & New Bridgeford and that I share that descent and that she may have carried that name until the day she wed my father; that she had a name and a story just as her mother had a name and a story, stories of a clan that had brothers and fighters and warriors and leaders, nurses and saints and piccolo players, and dear beautiful older sisters who pushed prams down hills and who went off to die in Melbourne with their unfathered babies—remember. May I remind you that her people are also my people, each day of my life I am telling their story too, that Richard King is a codename for Richard Wakefield. That I am also of my mother's people and that their story is mine, that I eat from a certain quality of china plate as a result of their misadventures and successes, that I can string a few words together with a semblance of sense thanks to their nurture.

hit out, he did not witness the Doctor's blows more tellingly returned, did not see the blood spurt out from the gullet—tomato relish red—nor did he note it spill down on the sun-cooked flesh like it was chutney.

He was off somewhere else involved in his own story. He was off having sex.

Chapter 34

Captain Naskin bravely marched through the havoc of mad and marauding convicts and soldiers, occasionally shooting

---

> May I urge you to remember that and may I as quickly, urge you to forget it.
>
> Because it's actually through my dad's Mum. She was a Manning, and her mother was a Quinn, you stick with the Quinns for about four generations and then you hook off to a Hopper. Stick with the Hoppers for a while then jump off when you get to the Hopper who married a Hooper. Mr Hooper's sister married a Wharton. She was Meredith Wharton. Her husband was a Wharton and her brothers-in-law were too. Her little girl was a Partridge but her sons were Whartons and so were their sisters until they got married. She's my Great-Great-Great how ever many Greats, Great-Great Something or Other. Her half-sisters were Sullivan. Her sisters were Partridges, VanderHaahs and Potters. Her mother had been a Fernandez but she changed her name too. Her step-sister was a Sullivan but her Pa wasn't, her father wasn't, her Da wasn't. He was a Naskin.
>
> And I proudly bear his given name.

this one or that one there, when and where it was required, like a man protected by an invisible shield. He made it to the hut he shared with the Spanish Girl. One may note at this time the odd one or two or three of the second echelon characters killed. Rantallion is shot or maybe crushed by a wagon, down with Beamish, this or that other one.

The Death of Governor Rantallion

'By Jesus.' Said Governor Rantallion. 'Another ruddy sad and little death.' The bitterful and pitiable and shitty death of your typical Britishman. 'Alone and afraid.' Contemptible and ever contemptuous. 'Cunts All.' Said Governor Rantallion or so he thought. He was mistaken in thinking that he had been speaking, but not either lip had pursed nor did his tongue ever rise. There was no motion to be had anymore about his body, all life had abandoned his bones and limbs and lips and pores with the arrival of the bullet, it was now all up to his brain and his heart to get this carriage through, to keep his soul alive, they would not suffice.

Governor Rantallion considered the unholy horror that had been wrought upon his person and he attended the bloody wound upon his chest and was stricken and aghast at the dire injury he there beheld. This was the not the stricken aghastness of the common layperson such as myself, your author, or may I respectfully suggest, a number of the readers/receivers of this passage. This was the stricken aghastness of a man who had had two years' training as a physician, he had for many years neglected the art but he hadn't forgot it. He knew precisely what peril this injury implied, and he knew to his advantage that he had approximately two minutes' time to correct this mortal danger and yet knew that to do so he would require certain thread and cloth which could perhaps be haphazarded together from items close by his person. He needed an astringent instantly and some form of infection retardant—preferably a lotion—within the half hour, a chest repressant would possibly be required and certainly a sling or hammock for his right arm. Lemon juice would suffice for an astringent as would gin which he indeed had upon his person in the leather-bound and silver-capped flask he had attached to his belt and surely boot polish would suffice as a lotion—no germ could stray a foothold in a swamp of polish—but he would require clean bandages within an hour and he would need a fine pair of tweezers to remove any bullet cinder that had sprayed about the wound. A general anaesthetic would certainly assist the patient's comfort. And curb his mounting panic. He needed water and sponges immediately, many towels and bandages, and the hands of a skilled surgeon, his own hands perhaps or those of the Doctor, oh the Doctor, away upon the bay, or the hands of a sensible man who could attend his instruction, and he then sadly reflected that he no longer had two minutes.

'Not yet.' Said Governor Rantallion, but not a word escaped his mouth nor, alas, another breath.

Captain Naskin was unable to assist Young Beamish in pulling Rantallion's body from under the cart, but he was at least pleased that in the enterprise he had elected to tug upon the left leg. Where Beamish positioned himself to pull upon the right put him directly in the passage of a bullet that caused his head to explode. Without Beamish's assistance, though with parts of his brain upon his tunic, Naskin thought it a fruitless endeavour to continue tugging vainfully upon the Governor's leg, particularly in such a dangerous location.

'Can I lend a hand?' Said the Colony Botanist/Portraitist as he crawled up to Captain Naskin and concealed himself against the upturned wagon, and then heard the quick crack and explosion of an old gum tree and he turned his head and when the Botanist saw the great flames come trooping down the hill, when he noticed the convicts enacting their evil and bringing perverse vengeance even closer to his stockade... (*he did certain things*)... till he was dead.

'Not me. You're on your own, Pal.' Replied Captain Naskin and he continued upon the journey back to his cabin. When he finally arrived at their hut he found a kurrapuuk-bewitched Spanish Girl sitting on the floor cast up against the wall like a rag doll, a five foot ten beautiful rag doll, a rag doll made out of flesh, flesh the colour of copper, and flesh that had never shown a flaw, not a blemish or imperfection in the time Naskin had known her except for those three splendid moles that went 'one two three' across her left breast. And the cheek-thing, of course. Flesh that had sweated this girl sodden. Her arms stretched up against the hot wall behind her, her brow and hair and clothing humid with perspiration, the fine white blouse wet and sheer against her chest, her skirts hitched up around her thighs, her bare legs and naked heels grinding relentlessly at the floor.

She was shaking and shuddering and sweating and shivering and, to Naskin's mind, panting like the Whore of Cairo.

This was not a common expression. It was not a popular allusion amongst the people of this time. It was not often said that *he/she or it is/was panting like the Whore of Cairo*. Not part of the general lingo.

It was a specific Captain Naskin thought.

He had had intercourse with a prostitute when his affairs had seen him to Egypt and he had noted the manner in which she panted. What the Spanish Girl was doing was like it.

And if we care to take exception to the lewd nature of Captain Naskin's thought we can perhaps at the same time, for a moment, excuse it. She was looking pretty damned lewd.

The Spanish Girl lifted her head up and it rolled for a moment, the bones in her neck seemed barely able to bear the burden. It nodded down towards her shoulder and then jerked away and then settled in what can, for our purposes, be called an approximation of up. She then put her fingers to her brow and frowned and ceased the senseless roll of her head and then shook it in despair. There was something lost here, there was something mad, there was something forfeited and bereaved and stolen from her, and she could not put her finger upon it. She frowned in confusion again, and she struggled between collapsing in despair on the one hand and thinking, thinking, thinking on the other, and only then did she remember to open her eyes.

'Fuck.' She thought. 'It certainly is a bright day.' She thought, 'And there's Captain Naskin.'

Her eyes hit him like a pair of javelins. When she blinked, he thought he'd die for losing them, when she opened them again he knew he'd drown. When she blinked again he knew what it would be like to face starvation, when she opened them he swooned in their bounty.

When he re-registered the rest of her—saw her panting on the floor, writhing in her hot sweat and heaving her wilful shanks around restlessly—and then remembered her standing with her small bag in the open doorway, saw her unlatching the cut on the chicken fence, pictured her poking at the tomato shoots with her stick, remembered her at night concentrating on her cards—saw her heaving her thighs around restlessly, writhing in her hot sweat and panting on the floor—he knew that he could live his life and not need to think much of any other thing. This was a new experience for Captain Naskin and it made him feel, what we would call, incredibly smushy.

When she spoke her voice was dry and crackled and harsh, it was the voice of a crone, she actually had to cough up a few bits of grit before she could find her key, and it seriously killed the mood.

'What's cooking?' She said.

'We're burning off all the kurrapuuks'

'Can't we eat some first?'

Captain Naskin was checking all the windows and securing the shutters. He was dragging the heavy table across to secure the door.

'You wouldn't want to go out there.'

'Doctor Wilmot said kurrapuuks make you go mad.'

'He didn't know the half of it.'

'Aren't you hungry?'

'I'm in the middle of a nightmare, Eva, I don't know what I'm feeling.'

It was the first time he'd ever said her name—Eva—and the effect hit them both—not like a bolt of lightning, not like an electric shock at all, but like a flood of golden molasses that was going to warmly smother them both. Smushy-like.

As we know, this was all completely new territory for Captain Naskin and after checking the windows a second time he could only conclude that how ever well or how ever poorly the battle between the prisoners and the soldiers was going, it seemed happy to play itself out some place else, and that the thing in this room, and the thing in his world, and the thing in this universe that should compel his attention is, was, and should be, the Spanish Girl.

He moved across the room towards her and sat down by her and stared before himself for a moment and fiddled with his bootlace. He breathed in deeply and immediately expelled the air from his lungs like he resented its presence in his body. He breathed in again, this time through his nostrils, and for the first time that afternoon got a whiff of those cooking kurrapuuks. 'Oh, Good God, what a smell.' He thought. 'So that's why everybody is so about themselves. Why it sates and it starves.'

He breathed in again, and sucked as much of that air in as could fill his body. He swooned in its smell and let it hold his back up.

When he sensed there was a person next to him he sat up straight and fussed with his cuffs, his head rolled around listlessly and, after he'd finally stilled it and could address some other purpose, he felt all sad and lost and bewildered and abandoned until he finally thought to open his eyes and he saw that it was Eva. When he saw that it was her he rested his eyes again and was eager to open them and affirm her presence. After resting them a third time he couldn't open them quick enough to remind himself that she was sitting here beside him, that it was beautiful her beside him, that it was she in this world, it was her here and now, and when he looked at her again he made sure he timed it with a really big inhale.

When he looked at her his two eyes hit her like a pair of javelins. She could have died at once by their regard, if she fell under their spell she would have surrendered her soul for eternity. When he fixed her in his dreamy stare she held she'd love every inch inside that man, and swear her days to his service. There's only one thing to do when you are besieged by such an onslaught of another person's appeal and that's to fight it back. She steadied her body to resist his temptation, she fumbled and moved restlessly and sought to steel her body with the support of her strong left arm and was delighted to find it in a position that so readily leant itself to this purpose, that she was, in fact, already leaning upon her strong left arm, all it required was a bit of strengthening. She straightened her pleats, and then fixed his eyes with every bit of power her facilities could muster. After they had held each other's stare for all of about ten or fifteen seconds, refuted each other's incursion, repelled each other's commanding assault, they both tacitly conceded that the other was quite a magnificent person.

They gently nestled with each other. Fumbled with the other's buttons. They drew back the fabric from the other's limbs. When she struggled his breeches down she discovered him already erect, when he entered her he discovered her already wet. When they felt the other one coming they noted themselves doing likewise and when they concluded they stared at each other for a long time and were surprised by what they felt. When he gently brushed her wet hair back from over her eyes she licked his wrist. It was a big lick. It ran up and onto his palm, poked around the webbing between his thumb and index finger and concluded as a soft kiss on his fingertips. He licked her back and it left her eyelashes glued together.

He leant his head against her left shoulder and kissed her forearm and she gently fiddled with the fine hairs at the nape of his neck and he noted five freckles upon her arm and was intrigued to detect that they were all arranged there like the Southern Cross. The Easternmost star had a tongue. No, it was a small supplementary freckle. A moon. A satellite. Or a remora. She had a fine scar that ran from the left and through her left shoulder freckle cluster, a thin white, luminescent wisp of a former injury.

He gently kissed the five freckles and nuzzled his face higher up her left arm and there noted a tattoo, a young rose about to open, a shy timorous bud, and he returned his attention to the astral freckles. 'What a shame people get tattoos.' He thought. 'When their bodies already have such wonderful stories upon them.' And then he sniffed the rose anyway and swooned gently as the smell of her sweet sweat bewitched him.

She rested her fingernails on his cheek and he clasped his hand behind her neck and they pulled their bodies together and they gently pressed their lips against each other's.

He sighed peaceably and the Spanish Girl joined his refrain and then she said, 'You truly are a remarkable, wonderful man Captain Naskin, in fact, the finest fellow that has e'er been known.' And he replied,

'Please, call me Richard.'

Unfortunately, by now Captain Richard Naskin had made himself a few too many enemies.

Chapter 35

Unfortunately, at that time when Captain Richard Naskin finally found himself at the end of his search and at the beginning of his journey, he had made himself just a few too many enemies. He had had a glorious awakening, he had suddenly seen the present and saw what that made of the past and was ready to stride into the future, to make a new start, but truth be told, he wasn't going anywhere yet. There were a few people who hadn't quite finished with him.

Outside things were calming down a bit. Once that first wave of bedlam had passed, a few of them in the midst of all this madness started to really consider their surroundings, not just the superficial things like the horses screaming and the buildings on fire and the profoundly delicious smell and the people shooting each other, but the more subliminal things— the anarchy, the confusion, the shifting fortunes of this battle being fought between the contained and the containees, the lack of order, the radical dismantling of the ruling system and the long term benefits that may promise, the will with which the prisoners were prolonging their liberty, the difficulty with which the soldiers were supressing it. If you had have been a prisoner at that time it would have taken a while for all these different ideas and themes and concepts to come into focus and crystallise and turn into the realisation that was *Good Bloody God, I'm Free*. Had you been there you would have stood slightly bewildered, set awry a moment, and desperately trying to remember what it was you had always told yourself you should do if ever you were granted your liberty. What it was you'd told yourself during those long hard months of incarceration, during that fourteen-month night of humiliation, pain and despair, what was that tiny candle you had always struggled to keep alight? What was that vain hope, that tiny forlorn promise, that bare skeleton of a dream you had granted to yourself?

This I say and this I swear on the grave of my mother, if I be a free child of England again, the first thing I'll do when at my liberty is . . . what?

Then you'd remember.

Good Bloody God, I'm Free. Great Bloody God. Hell. I'm free. What . . . what'll I . . . what to do? Jesus. What's the first thing I should do? You know this. You are one stupid person. You told yourself a thousand times. Oh that's right. Where are you Naskin, you bastard? I've got a bullet for you.

When it happened a lot of you would have got picked off pretty easy.

This was a new type of battle for the soldiers; it was not like the ones they had studied in training; it was not like ones they had fought to date. Here there was no orderly advance from a well-drilled phalanx of pikemen, no diversionary sorties by a force of fleet-footed archers, no Prussians on horseback. This battle did not obey the rules of any battle they'd learnt and studied and fought but that's not to say it didn't have rules of its own.

The soldiers soon learnt that one of the rules was that these prisoners seemed to set fire to more things than any other enemy they had ever heard of.[5] Rule two was that when a convict suddenly pauses mid-action, stands up straight and

---

[5] One can hardly blame the convicts for turning into a bunch of pyromaniacs. They were Europeans. In Europe fire is the fourth element you are taught about, it is the last one you remember. In Europe fire is a small thing, it is an occasionally hazardous thing but it is a mostly domesticated thing, it is a utility. The European knows of the mighty history of the wind, they see daily the mighty conflict that rages between earth and sea, their countries shake to mighty impulses and tempests of land and air and water. But fire? It is a candle, it is a wick. Barely an element at all.

Not in Australia sister.

The sun sends that fire down like its got enough to burn every bit of skin from your body and it's bloody well right. The earth grabs that fire up and sends it straight back barrelling up your legs, there are times when my homeland just cannot be stood upon. Its vain and desperate inhabitants try to dance halfway up in the air, it's more sensible inhabitants keep in the shade. This place is an oven, an unholy heat and lord you should see this place when a wee flame takes hold. That's when you get a full appreciation of why fire gets to call itself a fully fledged element. All the other elements have clearly agreed to stand back and let fire do its thing. Wind has agreed to occasionally lend a hand, to give fire a nudge here and there to create these magnificent tunnels down which fire can hurtle its grasp. Water basically keeps enough land from escaping to ensure fire has a stage, it flourishes in small pockets, feeds some small gasps of life. And earth has long ago resigned itself to being whipped wicked, it nurtures where it can (mainly in and around Cobram), it bears the unholy fire in those places where all is lost.

The convicts weren't to know any of this.

They probably pictured a few prettily burning carts, the Lord's barn crackling and crashing down wearily upon itself, the Bastille going up in an emancipating glow.

Wrong, wrong, wrong.

They got hell.

with a sweet dopey grin starts staring around themselves in bewilderment, that's a pretty good time to shoot 'em.

That was how Stanton went down. He stood straight up like an idiot, thought, *'Eh that's right. Where's that rogue Naskin?'*, looked around and got a bullet in his head.

Moll Furnham had just dragged a pistol and purse from a young dead corporal when she stood to full height, thought, *'That Naskin'll be close arounds'* and looked North then West and as far as South-West when a bullet blew her head and bloodied bonnet eight foot high.

Same with Pentridge. Stood up and thought, *'Oi Naskin, you'd want to be running fast, Good God, what's this explosion of blood around my waist?'* and pippity-pip, his upper body was blown off by a dozen bullets.

It was a bit different with Young Collins. *'Now . . . where's a boat?'* and then a bullet through the back of his neck, just below his hairline.

But some of them survived long enough to begin the execution of their plan. To drag themselves shy of the fierce fury of the battle, to retreat from its centre, to pass to its edges, to draw back from the fire and start thinking about coming up with a way of hunting down Captain Naskin without realising that they had been doing precisely that. The retreat from the heart of the battle had taken them directly upon that trail passed by Captain Naskin some half an hour previously, unknowingly they had found themselves stumbling in his footsteps, in fact, retreating directly to his door. This event occurred to about twenty of them at exactly the same time. It was rather dramatic, this realisation that this building they were trying to hide themselves behind actually contained the very object of their endeavour—it took a while to process.

For some it was the sudden mysterious remembering that this was Captain Naskin's house, for others it was the fact that they had remembered seeing him walking this way just near half an hour ago, for others it was the glimpse of him through the window lying naked and still and at peace in the arms of the beautiful naked Spanish Girl.

CHAPTER 36

Naskin heard something that woke him up. He then heard about 18–20 other somethings. It was just like that, it wasn't *eighteen to twenty*, it was *18–20*. This was data to Captain Naskin. He reached for his gun.

He was up and had checked the windows and was back down in the time you'd have blinked and had established the positions and weaponry and the vague identity of most of them. None of them liked him. He knew that if he stayed where he was he'd be able to kill ten of them however if he rolled under the table and fired from there he'd only kill seven but it would be a better seven to kill. He knew that his primary objective was to save the Spanish Girl. He urged her be still, shy and silent and Good God she took some quietening. He knew that there could be no battle here. He knew he'd have to walk out there unarmed and surrender himself to their vengeance. He knew he'd have to forfeit his life to save this girl and he knew he'd do it.

He was about to do so when he suddenly wondered whether he especially liked the idea of surrendering Eva to the company of these twenty convicts, four in particular, without somehow being around to keep an eye on things. He most certainly did not like the idea.

He had to rethink and he had to rethink fast and he didn't have time because they'd just set fire to his house.

Chapter 37

'I told you fella you never even looking in my eyes.'

Miles away, Young Corporal Robertson was having something of a life-defining moment of his own. He had initially been delighted when he had been appointed to command the expedition to make contact with the Portuguese— he swore to himself that he would not err nor fail in that mission and consequently commend himself to a number of people (the Governor certainly and the Spanish Girl perhaps by dint of his valour) and yet the more he considered his situation, the more he could not help but conclude that in that endeavour he had failed most miserably. He had not been able to make sense of the maps, his soldiers were dying or dead, their provisions had been too quickly depleted, there was not water where the charts swore it, he was now twelve days into a mission he had been assured would want only three, and there were no Portuguese. He had struggled for four hours to transform his body from a prone, wretched and lifeless pitiable object to a wretched and weak feeble thing with the stench of death about it. He was making progress, but he was making damned slow progress. 'Water.' He gasped. 'Water.' He rasped weakly and he rued that we Englishmen had not had the foresight to make it a monosyllabic word. 'Kaah.' He said. He wondered how the word would sound in Portuguese and then wondered whether he himself would ever make contact with the Portuguese, he wondered whether he would be treated kindly or feared by the Portuguese and the more he thought about the Portuguese the more he compelled your author to do likewise. Have I explained the Portuguese? Have I made it clear why Young Robertson's out here dying in the desert?

The story 'Carrion Colony' will exist and has already existed in a number of forms. There is the treatment version and the outline version and the first and second and the 'multitude of drafts' version, there is the strictly bowdlerised and ruthlessly paraphrased version I explain to anyone who asks me about my novel, there shall soon be the movie version and the mini-series version, this novelic version will be praised for being the most exacting, the viewmaster version cherished for being the most aptly edited, the operatic version will be treasured for being the most stirring, the spoken word version shall be celebrated for the quality of John Hurt's exemplary elocution and the Lloyd Webber musical version shall be dismissed as 'a boring piffle'. None of them are a piece of piss compared to the campfire version. In the campfire version there's a whole extra fifty minutes of storytelling about the Portuguese and their significance is explained and extrapolated upon. About how they may have been spotted by some convicts out hurling peat, how some natives were 'visited' by some great 'islands of wood and cloud' that had come into their bay and had markings that suggested the flag of Portugal. In the campfire version a great deal is made about the arrival of the Portuguese—I sing a song and there is a short dance—it all alarms Governor Rantallion considerably and he imposes an immediate curfew and rallies as many armed men to the defence of the colony as he can muster. He decides to send a deputation to make contact with the sailors from Portugal but, wishing to keep his best soldiers within his vicinity and available for his defence, he concocts this deputation out of a vain rattle-tag of soldiers, a mishap of men, a pitiable torn of misshapen miscreants, and he appoints as their commander a tadpole. Consistent with his strategy in the operating theatre, he was ridding this land of scruff, he was clearing the turf of scurf. In one of the most harrowing and heartbreaking moments in the story of 'Carrion Colony' we learn that he equips Young Corporal Robertson—Young Corporal Robertson mind you who is still at this point of the narrative the darling beau of the Dear Spanish Girl—and these men not with the maps that describe these outlying lands but with the maps that are intended for the Portuguese. With the maps that describe non-existent waterholes, the maps full of false tracks and booby traps, the maps of poison lands that—in his best case scenario—would be prised from the dead grasp of the skeletal deputation, prised out of the dead fists of the valiant English boys by the inquisitive Portuguese and they would read there writ 'Fuck Off Frogs'. In no uncertain terms. So splendid and compelling is this moment of narrative and high drama that you unfailingly swear each further day of your life to the destruction of the vile, bastardly and hateful Governor Rantallions (read John Howards) of this world but that's the campfire version. It also has a whole lot of stuff about a colony cook that contains the following passage:

Our Bennelong took the fruit and held it up before his face and inspected it for a moment. This fruit was the size of a coconut and was the shape of a pear, it had the skin of an avocado and was a colour that had never existed on this continent until the Europeans arrived—not in the feather of any bird, the bruise of any injury, the eye of any creature, not in the depth of any pool. It was the rich and deep lustre of a certain purple in shadow. He cut a small nick in its skin with his thumbnail and then held the fruit above his upturned face and sucked out its flesh and juice, leaving the skin exhausted and empty. 'Look up there at that possum with his three little ones. Good fellow, hey?' He said, and the Colony Astronomer was astonished that Our Bennelong could discern the gender of a possum at a distance of at least three score and ten feet. In the dark. Our Bennelong spat the many pips into his palm and licked the stray drips of juice that had run down his forearms. It was the way a savage would eat, so UN-European, thought the Colony Cook. It was ungodly, heathen, in harmony with the food and eating it the way food should be eaten, it was sensuous, intimate, respectful and honourable and conducted in a state of worship and grace and the Colony Cook abhorred it. He preferred the European way of eating, nailing and hammering the food to a stark white plate, staking it out and stabbing it and searing it and dissecting it with his cool instruments, spreading it out and succouring it like it was prey, like it was booty, like it was tithe, commanding it and defacing and subjugating it and pasting it together and rendering it a pollution, a fetid mush of fat and oil and grease and dripping, and then embarrassingly secreting it into his mouth. His food would leave his body as a vile secretion and that's the way it would enter him why it was only proper. In one passage it would go as a rancid poison and out the other orifice it would so pass.

But that's really all you need to know about the Colony Cook and perhaps it's a bit much at that. There's also a rather expansive riff that ultimately leads nowhere about the convicts singing during the last days of imprisonment in England and on the ships transporting them to their new home.

Understand that this was not a very choral period in England's history. Perhaps when a stranger passed by a stall holder might sing a brief inventory of his wares, a few lines of a tired old chant, a lazy song of praise or pun upon his wares ('Gather for ye pots, I've pots and more pots'), there were priests who sang, or intoned I suppose is more the word, but not much general singing. Certainly not amongst these types of people.

These were people who had come from the gutters and fetters and sewers of all of London and all of England. Places where people lived eighty to the alley and sixty below a bridge, where they bedded down forty to a room in cold dark basements on rotting boards amongst rogues and whores and rutting scum and paid a hard-earned penny for the honour. Hardly the place to spontaneously burst out in song.

These people were thieves, they were pickpockets and burglars and murderers. They stalked you sharply in the marketplace, they squatted waiting for hours upon your rooftops, in the dark beneath your stair. Not people likely to pass their time belting out a hearty song, rhapsodising harmonically and clapping their hands.

Amongst their company there were many who had not in their lives sung a single note.

But get them in that boat, chuck them in those chains and cast them out and away from England forever and for forever and a day and you could not stop the people from singing.

Never mind that their descendants would prove to be the most sorry nation of mean-spirited and bigoted wretches (under John Howard's Leadershit) the world has ever had befoul its surface, for a time at least there was grand glory inside these people's hearts. There was joy and irony and happy resignation in their song:

Farewell to Old England forever,
Farewell to my rum culls as well,
Farewell to the well known Old Bailey,
Where I used for to cut such a swell.

This was emancipation for these people. They were suddenly free to live their lives out in the open. Not to have to hide their life away behind a whole host of lies and code names and secrets but to live their life out in the open where everyone could see them and know who they were. To be as grand as they could be. Sure they were prisoners, low convicts, but for the first time in their lives they were out in the open. It was like sunshine. And they sang funny, bittersweet, clever songs to announce themselves to the world.

Taint leaving Old England we cares about,
Taint cos we mis-spells what we knows.
But because all we light fingered gentry,
Hops around with a log on our toes.

When they got to Australia, when they beheld the perverse and corrupted foliage, the bizarre and abject wildlife, the sorry and disreputable trees and poor gullies and belaboured Aborigines, not one of them ever sung another word.

It is explained that the Colony Cartographer noted the disingenuous maps with which the deputation were equipped and in vain sought to arm them with contrary charts. How he bravely tried to smuggle his more accurate reckonings of the land to the deputation through an intermediary. We learn how Jack Robinson rebuffed the entreaty by saying, 'What am I, my brother's keeper?' and then laughed sourly at the particular irony of that remark. In the campfire version, the rock attack upon the Spanish Girl actually occurs on the Woman-billeting Wednesday somehow. There is a whole 'nother section that describes the burgeoning relationship of Naskin and the Spanish Girl; Anka Salim, the Arab Convict, makes it here if he doesn't find himself a spot elsewhere; the Second to the Quarter-Master is expanded upon and there is a character who shouts 'Rabbit Skins. Line up for your Rabbit Skins'. None of it makes it into the novel. It is explained how Young Corporal Robertson coud be alone and in a desert at least four and perhaps as many as twelve days into an ill-fated mission and yet still be present at a card game that apparently occurred at Jack Robinson's the night before, a lens grinder has his tooth removed, and it all makes sense that these affairs all occurred three weeks before a week after Young Corporal

Robertson had left for America. Someone's donkey falls in a trench. In the campfire version the now nigglesome distinction I have got going about Old Bridgeford as opposed to New Bridgeford is explained away once and for all and finally and to the satisfaction of all.

For receivers of the significantly inferior novelic version of 'Carrion Colony' it simply suffices that you understand that Young Corporal Robertson was away and in the middle of a desert abandoned by his fellows and burning to death. Poor soul. In the novelic version of 'Carrion Colony' this information and the affairs that led to it had to be hidden away somewhere—here will do. Young Corporal Robertson had somehow extricated himself from the mad events that would unfold in Old & New Bridgeford but he had somehow got himself into a stickier situation indeed, it was out of the frying pan into the fire again with Young Corporal Robertson—will this fellow never learn?

Chapter 38

'I told you fella you never even looking in my eyes.'

Miles away, Young Corporal Robertson was having something of a life-defining moment of his own. He had struggled for four hours to transform his body from a prone, wretched and lifeless pitiable object to a wretched and weak feeble thing with the stench of death about it. He was making progress, but he was making damned slow progress. 'Water.' He gasped. 'Water.' He rasped weakly. 'Kaah.' He was going to die, he knew it, unless he could somehow manage to rest his chin up on his elbow. If he could only lick that grain of sand from his lip, if he could just feel sense in that one little toe there, then perhaps he could commence the three-day hike back to the waterhole. He decided that it all depended on whether he would be able to get that one little finger to twitch. Boom, then his leg exploded with a violent spasm, the eruption grabbed the other leg and shook it, his arm flew out wildly, and his whole body heaved itself up and over.

Damn, he thought, his body shuddering in vague aftershock. *Got myself face up*. For all his exciting and rather exhausting moving around he had succeeded only in transforming himself from a tight defensive cove with its back turned to the sun to a frail little paper doll pinned to a hot plate. He wearily opened his eyes, a movement that caused his head to melt. He closed them promptly, reeling at the blow the explosion of light had delivered, wondering that it had a black head in the middle of it, madly trying to revive his tear ducts. He furrowed his brow and by that action cast a shadow over his smoking eye jelly and could not help wondering about that little black head. He was about to throw caution to the wind and open his eyes again when his foot started twitching uncontrollably. He thought about going with the insane foot twitch, couldn't really see where that could lead, so he elected to throw the aforesaid caution to the wind and he opened his eyes.

Lo, there was a black head.

There was Our Bennelong. He understood now. That explained all the problems he'd been having with his leg. It was Our Bennelong shaking it the whole time. *Aahh.* He could relax now. Our Bennelong slapped him across the face, dragged him for four hours over the rough and rocky ground and then threw him down roughly into the shade of that region's only tree. Our Bennelong stabbed at the roots and cupped the water it yielded and splashed it upon Young Robertson's face. He smeared cool mud on his burning limbs, he dripped juice upon his baked tongue, he pissed clean the dust from Young Robertson's mouth in accordance with a tribal remedy which Robertson didn't really hold was completely necessary. He healed him.

He struggled up a fire and then blew gentle smoke upon Corporal Robertson that repaired and roused his body till he was ready to eat. The smoke that had arisen Young Robertson was the smoke that curled from a steak of kurrapuuk meat that Our Bennelong had got cooking over the fire, it revived Robertson at the moment that it was most opportune to be et, he let the blood spill freely down his chin. He blinked and shook the salt from his skin. He looked sleepily at old Our Bennelong and he seeped gratitude from his pores.

'You think I'm stupid?' Said Our Bennelong and Young Robertson answered,

'No I think you are magnificent, you just saved my life, God praise you.'

'You think I'm just some silly chin-wag.'

'Not for a moment.'

'Why you walking out in the middle of nowhere?'

'I beg your pardon.'

'Why you walking in the middle of nowhere. I seen you, you're walking backwards and forwards.'

'I was lost.'

'I'd told you which way to go.'

'We never discussed this.'

'I told you stories. I told you, fella, you never even looking in my eyes.'

'I'm sure I have, many times. They're brown.'

'I told you this whole land.'

'Lies, damned lies.'

'I told you all about this our home. Is Namanook the snake climbing up this coast. He's the snake who's reaching.'

'Yes, well you told me about him.'

'Why do you think I'm telling you these stories?'

'I don't know. I was too polite to interrupt. They were odd stories about body markings and matters akin.'

'They were how you going to get there. The whole snake is a body, is a map, it's lying on the treetops, its sleeping in the valley.'

'You kid me.'

'It's your life, fellow. Only way you breathe.'

'But this was all some meandering story about how the wombats got their coarse brown fur and their little, squinty eyes. It had nothing to do with life and treetops and me breathing. It was about some giant snake...'

'Namanook.'

'Yes him, and some wombats fighting for some emu eggs. Have you just said that?'

'Oh that just a pretty story makin' sure of the children. Making sure they pay attention, getting a remember for the information.'

'I see. So it was a mnemonic.'

'Yes I called him him. Namanook. I tipped you off proper, brother. You don't know your Shakespeare.'

'Well it all sounded so unpertinent. I didn't realise it was in code. I apologise.'

'Is how you going to get there fellow.'

'Well, tell it again.'

'You just follow them there little bushes them is the tail's tip they going to take you up his body get you to where your Portuguese tribe are.'

'How will I know I'm going the right way?'

'You going to have to watch youself, when you sliding up a snake's belly you at danger fella. You take one wrong step he's going to give you the eye and reach around and swallow you down.'

'I'll be careful.'

'You can slide up his greasy skin or you can be snatched up by his jaws.'

'I'll watch for the jaws.'

'This land is a snake I'm telling you. You got to watch for his fangs they're snapping at you they can snatch you up.'

'And do these fangs also have a geographical counterpart?'

'On the second morning you going to see a creek down a valley to your father's side. What do you think you're going to do?'

'I imagine I'll be hot and tired and I'll race down for a drink.'

'How do you think you'd go at fighting a crocodile big as a canoe?'

'I don't know.'

'How do you think you'd go against fifteen?'

'I'd be hopeless.'

'Namanook the Snake's got horror fangs you stay clear of them, he's armoured up, he's fighting with them wombats, you watch for his poison spur.'

'Tell me about the poison spur.'

'It's about three days' walk up on this fellow, you'll find the place you'll just walk yourself there. You'll be well buggered and you'll come across a stream. You drink from there and you only get to walk for another half a day, that's it for you fellow. If you stop yourself from drinking you'll get yourself to the milk sacs by nightfall. There you'll sleep easy, it's a mountaintop.'

'It's not an especially high mountain is it?'

'Next morning you'll see yourself a gully. If you walk down that gully you'll be straight in the snake's belly.'

'I will eschew the snake's belly.'

'No you get straight in there fella. You stay there for a while, him not squeezing you. Him squeezing turtles and kurrapuuks and kangaroos. You stay there a couple of days, you, and your company, you eating plenty. Him never squeeze you.'

'Surely there'll be savages?'

'Prithee, I beg your pardon.'

'Surely if this place is so abundant we'll encounter proprietorial savages.'

Our Bennelong paused at that moment, he arched his cruelly scarred and sunburnt brow; he picked at the pale flecks of paint that marked his cheeks. He looked away at the horizon, he seemed to be trying to remember something—perhaps whether there were in fact savages in the belly of the snake, whether they were dangerous and proprietorial. He frowned and shook his head, sighed once, and scraped his long fingers through the dirt and by the coincidence of the action, after a long sweep of his hand across the dusty ground, had herded about ten or twenty pebbles together at his fingertips where his hand came to rest. He picked them all up and thoughtfully bounced them in his hand until one by one they escaped that makeshift trampoline and in time he was juggling naught but air. Whatever on earth he was going to say next he clearly considered it to be very important. When he finally spoke he stared Young Robertson threateningly in the eye and spoke slowly and surely and with a deep dry voice that rasped with the harsh and dusty fire of this land and which boomed with the resonant chorus and authority of the thousands of his ancestors who had made this land their own.

'I've started to understand what you fellas is callin' us when you use that word, you stick to calling us natives.'

'Natives, yes sure, Aborigines, Pidginese-indigenies, whatever, will we encounter any troublesome types?'

'It just the Nunawading folk. They keep an eye on you sure but you do right and move on they mind their business.'

'Right. So where to from there?'

'From there on in you riding on his back you stick to those cliffs there on this hand you going to be ridin' up and ridin' down, you sliding there backwards and sidewards you won't even notice a thing the ride's *that* fast. You'd never of thought a man could walk so far without even tiring.'

'It's that easy?'

'You'll be sliding to your Portugal Man.'

'Look, why don't you just take me there?'

'I got other things to do.'

'Well then, I want to get it very, very clear where I turn left.'

'I never said you turn left.'

'You did... I thought you did. What did you say?'

'I'm not telling you again. This is what I'm saying, you didn't even listen. Never do.'

'I did listen, it's a truth, I swear it. You said turn off left near the cliffs, I think... Can you just say it again?'

'This is what you think about me all the time. That I'm a child 'cause I'm not all done up in your red waistcoats and white breeches. You'll learn it's too hot here for much more than what I've got on. You're just thinking I'm a hobbledehoy because I'm not dressed in your fire and ice. You're spitting on me.'

'No, really I'm not, I'm sorry if it appears that way. I was really listening, very intently, but I just missed it. *Something something something—left*... then you mumbled.'

'I never mumbled.'

'Well I clearly remember you doing so.'

'I never said left.'

'I'm sure you did. *From there on in you riding on his back you stick to those cliffs there on your left.*'

'No I waved my hand.'

'That's right you did. You're right, you did. I'm sorry. Which hand was it?'

'I showed you once.'

'It was too dark.'

'No it wasn't you weren't paying attention.'

'Well I thought I was, you just unexpectedly started doing hand actions.'

'See... that's when your people and my people...'

'Honestly it isn't. Honestly—man to man—I just didn't notice what happened when your hand went off. Can you do it again? Please.'

Our Bennelong did.

CHAPTER 39

Naskin heard something that woke him up. He then heard about 18–20 other somethings. It was just like that, it wasn't *eighteen to twenty*, it was *18–20*. This was data/datum to Captain Naskin. He reached for his gun.

He was up and back down in the time you'd have blinked and had established the positions and weaponry and the vague identity of most of them. None of them liked him. He knew that if he stayed where he was he'd be able to kill ten, however if he rolled under the table and fired from there he'd only kill eight but it would be a better eight to kill.

'You're shivering.' Said Eva and Captain Naskin quietly hushed her be still. He willed her to silence with an urgent wave of his hand and by pointing his pistol at her throat. He held her still with an unrelenting stare that scared the skin off her so she shut right up and waited until he gave a quick nod and she said, 'Here, can I get you a blanket I can't believe you could be cold its so...' and Captain Naskin shook his head and put his finger before his lips and he cooed. She held her tongue until he gave her a wink and then she said,

'Well I can't be bothered trying to work out what's the matter with you, you can bloody well freeze.'

And Captain Naskin whispered,

'Eva, you know enough of the word "shiver" to know that it may have two similar but slightly different meanings?'

'What's your point?' She said.

'One can shiver because one is cold or one can shiver because one is afeard for his life.'

'And you were shivering because... '

'I am not cold.'

'Then...'

'One can shiver because one fears one's life is in considerable peril.'

'And you shivered?'

'Aye, I shivered.'

'What's your point?'

'I did not shiver for either of those reasons.'

'Finally. There is a third shiver?'

'It is a thing a gentleman might feel after having spent time with a lady. A pleasant settling of the shoulders and a gentle tremor along the spine.'

'It is a splendid tingle?'

'Indeed, an involuntary jolting of the body that faintly echoes the pleasantries they have shared, a momentary recall so delightful that it sets the whole body a shudder and that could be taken for a shiver. However, I do have some matters to attend to with some persons outside so if you'll excuse me...'

'Can I help?'

'Perhaps.' Captain Naskin replied and he turned and grabbed a second pistol and Eva for the first time noticed the great oriental dragon that was inked in to the man's left shoulder blade and the great spitting panther upon its right counterpart with which it made dispute. 'But maybe on this first occasion I might just try a few things of my own.'

He was up and back down in the time you'd have blinked. He knew that his primary objective was to save the Spanish Girl and he knew that she'd be in considerable peril if a whole lot of bullets were going to start flying around particularly if Young Waters was going to be firing off from behind that tree where he appeared to have finally settled, he thought, he'll shoot her with probably his eighth, actually seventh shot and I can't hide her anywhere else, they've built this house too small damn them. He knew that there could be no battle here. He knew he'd have to walk out there unarmed and surrender himself to their vengeance. He wished he had his trousers on. He knew he'd have to forfeit his life to save this girl and he knew he'd do it.

He was about to do so when he suddenly wondered whether he especially liked the idea of surrendering Eva to the company of these twenty convicts, four in particular, without somehow being around to keep an eye on things. He most certainly did not like the idea.

He had to rethink and he had to rethink fast and he didn't have time because they'd just set fire to his house.

Chapter 40

'Good Lord. What's going on?' Said John Dunnock and he sidled up to Doctor Wilmot and he gently pressed him in the ribs. 'What the fuck is that sound?' He asked politely.

Doctor Wilmot fell to his knees and clenched his fists in anguish. He knew in an instant what that sound was and it nearly rendered his bones apart. He fell abjectly to the ground in the company of those gentlemen and he wailed at their feet. Doctor Wilmot could not sweat out his grief, he could not weep out his horror, and he could not later piss out his despair, there was no dispelling this immense torment from his body except by the use of words and so he turned in the direction of Old & New Bridgeford and he roared his anguish to the waves,

'And it's all of you, God damn you. You don't know what you've done.'

He heard the cries of individual birds, individual birds that he had specifically befriended, specific birds who had ate from his hand, who had brought him berries in their beaks, who had let him approach their nests, let guard their brood, let courier their eggs, he heard *their* cries of agony, he heard their desperate plea for pity, their last appeals for mercy come a-pealing across the choppy bay. Heard their cries of horror and pain as they had the rock thrust down on their bony legs to secure their body upon the ground, and then had their head jiggled around roughly until the thing finally came off. There is no describing those cries of suffering.

It was partly like the sound of any creature of this earth staring oblivion in the eye, it was partly like the sound of about a dozen ice cubes being bounced about upon a trampoline. He heard the death cries of their chicks.

'And you are all in on this. All of you planned this.' Wept Young Doctor Wilmot. 'All of you will be damned.' He fell abjectly to the ground in the company of those gentlemen and he wailed at their feet.

He even heard the last death cry, Doctor Wilmot heard the last peals, heard the screams, heard the desperate prayers for mercy, of the one he had taken to calling Laurence, who had once slumbered aside the Doctor's arm, who had been with him and been his ally that day when they had had to fight off the goanna, the one of them squawking and dive bombing from the trees, the other (the Doctor) swinging his leather attaché case and shooing it away with the branches, the one Laurence who had occasionally mistaken the Doctor's lower leg for a kurrapuuk hen. He heard Laurence's cry as that bird died and he knew enough about the kurrapuuk's one hundred and sixty-four calls to know that this was a new one, a cry he had never heard before and he knew precisely what that bird said. It chilled his bones, it rallied to predominance the jelly in his kneecaps, it left him stricken. It was,

'For Pity's Sakes where is Big John, the newest kurrapuuk?'

'I damn you all.' Said Young John Wilmot the Doctor as he shuddered on the ground and sought to gouge his fingernails from his very fingertips. 'I damn you all.' He said as he knelt servile before the sun and tried to scratch his very eyeballs from their very sockets. And old John Dunnock the Very Cobbler said,

'I reckon that must be the sound of a thousand cartwheels all stopping off at once.'

'God damn you, Drudge.' Said the Doctor. 'That is the bird-killing. They are the birds crying. That is the cry of us killing this land.' And he pushed John Dunnock in his frail, hollow chest sending the silly old hermit flailing away backwards. He kicked the old coot in the back, which sent the old shit-tosser sliding along the harsh rock about twelve feet to a drop of about five feet onto a crop of jagged and brittle shards. He grabbed the old arse-harvester by the shoulders and back-pedalled him about eighteen feet and then crushed him down into the sand, the sand that gathered in a relatively sheltered bit of this rock, he ground Mad John's head back till it reached hard rock beneath the slight lay of sand and until his neck bled by dent of sheer extension and he said,

'They're killing this land. We have come here with a sword not a thresher.'

And he wept and he panted and he beat his fists upon John Dunnock's forehead and ears and face and he roared again, 'No, not a thresher.' As his fingers gently encircled John Dunnock's thin neck.

Fortunately for John Dunnock, this was the part of the rock where he had made his camp, assembled his meagre possessions, where he would nightly rest his head. And as we know, Dunnock had him a knife on that there island. And as surely as scissors beats paper and paper beats rock, as we all learnt in childhood, knife beats fingers.

Chapter 41

'Wacko.' Thought Captain Naskin. 'Here's an opportunity.'

Captain Naskin smiled at Eva and whispered her to be very, very still, he urged her delay without fear until the flames were widespread enough to conceal his actions. He bid she defer her mad panic, he entreated her to trust him and be patient. In the meantime he was going to have a bit of a go at picking off as many convicts as he could. He skipped from window to window, keeping an eye on the flames and keeping an eye on the fellows outside. He took one bullet in the shoulder but he delivered seven that stopped hearts beating.

And they were the seven he most wanted to get. And one of those seven bullets that Captain Richard Naskin fired off that afternoon took Convict No. 25 in the chest and caused mad and sufficient injury about Convict No. 25 to leave that person distraught—nay significantly distressed—nay—to the eye, stone cold dead. He got it all out of his system.

Chapter 42 Convict No. 25

There was one amongst their company, a one so wretched and vile of intent that their type would be known to the contemporary reader. There has not in these past one hundred and seventy years been such a merry and such a miraculous and happy dance within the human gene pool such that we have seen these sly and horrid creatures extinguished. We have not evolved that rapidly. Bridewell is a cranky bugger, Robertson's a twit. You may have friends or companions or colleagues who vaguely approximate these characters, I certainly do—they're no great problem, humanity can accommodate them, humanity can endure them. Cunts like Convict No. 25 are a completely different kettle of fish. They hurt too many people, they upset too many people, they generate too much hatred, cause too much rancour in other people's hearts. I am confident that any damn reader who has persisted thus far, be it in whatever language, be they field worker, scout or musician, store-strutman or scrape, will know of at least one person as wretched, faithless and contemptible as Convict No. 25 and if you're a reader who is a friend or intimate of the author you'll certainly know who I'm talking about. Convict No. 25 who enjoys the dual distinction of being the most despicable inhabitant of Old & New Bridgeford and concurrently the most loathsome and most nefarious person my pen can write, had this habit of sometimes hunching in both shoulders whilst talking and in so doing brought you intimately closer to the conversation, lent it a Byzantine character, lent it whispers, made it feel like you were conspiring, made it feel unclean.

We are not free of the characters of old, we have not cast off the great stories of heroes or tyrants, there are still jezebels and cowards and wretches and pillagers around and about and amongst us, they stand beside us on our trams, they answer our calls, sell us our purchases, clean our streets and meet us at taverns and they concur with our suggestion that we buy them a drink. There are still vessels in which we can pour out our stored up and overflowing reserves of hatred and venom. Where we can pour out our hate and pour out our hat and shamelessly vilify and damn our contemporaries, where we can publicly and to our friends and colleagues and on whatever stage or page we find, damn and slander our enemies, tear their lives to shreds, humiliate them and publicly cast their secrets to the scrutiny of the world because we all know people still hate, we all still hate sometimes. We all still know how good it can feel to let a little bit of that poison out, let a little bit out in whatever form and however it helps, and in ways calculated to impair our enemy. Isn't man a wonderful thing—we have evolved up from the reptiles but our souls have not entirely forgot them.

About Convict No. 25.

Moll Furnham had heard that Convict No. 25 had had some marvellous affair with some man of letters while she was still in England but the affair had somehow imploded into a mad chaos that had blasted his charmed life tragically awry. 'Twas said the man of letters often spoke of his former paramours in such terms. Old Nulihan had heard a whisper that Convict No. 25 had engineered a coach accident when learning of his beloved's condition and somehow, in trying to avert the likely course of the latter, averted the likely course of the former. Steered the coach into a tree and ensured he caused safe injury to the two of them, but made sure there was plenty trouble for passenger number three. It was said that Convict No. 25 had not been the matron she purported, had not been a man of honour—he had dissembled, the confidant he had suggested, the unpoisoned lover that a man could assume.

'Twas known by a few that Convict No. 25 had accidentally left some papers on a carriage, and they were discovered and consequently published and whilst he had wished greater edit to their contents he could not achieve nor conceptualise the means by which he could arrest their committal to ink and he had barely imagined the unchivalrous hurt they would cause to a number of essentially honourable people. He knew that he had not shown 'form'. He knew about 'form'. He had read about it in books. No one would read about it in his. 'Twas the word that Convict No. 25 had slit four farmers up the belly in the night and pulled their livers out their throat and left them dangling from their mouths. Whatever Convict No. 25 had done I find the 'doings' of Captain Naskin a lot more interesting.

Chapter 43

When Captain Naskin adjudged the flames a-high enough and the beams threatened to fall and the windows had exploded and the heat was damned fierce—the smoke itself would have certainly ensured that not much of what was going on inside could be seen outside had he cared to notice—Captain Naskin commenced removing some floorboards.

Captain Naskin was the type of man who saw the value in a good hole beneath one's house. When the carpenters and the press gang of convicts had built him his cottage he thanked them for their labour and for the glass in his windows, he admired the chim-chimney and he tested the strength of the walls. He kicked at the nails in the floorboards and then yelled at them to depart. He then waited for nightfall, and began adding a hole. He didn't know what this hole would be for, he knew it could be useful. Perhaps one day to hide treasure, maybe a cache of weaponry, the way he had been behaving of late, it might one day prove a grave, he didn't know for sure, but he held it could come in handy.

Captain Naskin was the kind of man who can dig a hole really quickly.

Three nights did not want for the task and he spent the next three nights wishing it hadn't been so quick to dig. He considered digging another. He spent the next three nights planing its walls until they were as sheer as a plank and was putting in shelving when he decided to turn it into a tunnel. A tunnel that ran straight out the back and emerged in the bush land near the cliff side by Westerfold's Creek where he built a path. He'd left a neat pile of gold buried near the roots of the wattle tree where he'd remember to come back for it.

They all watched the flames engulf that small house, tear it asunder, and then dump it contemptuously down in an explosion of dust and smoke; the convicts danced and hooted it up at the site, they spat and pissed at the flames, they warmed their bare arses with its heat and Captain Naskin and Eva sitting on the cliffside both agreed it was a rather thrilling spectacle. They even sat around and watched a bit more of the battle played out before them—disingenuously rued the loss of this or that possession—and when they decided they couldn't work out which way it was going to go, and when those flames looked like they were just about to get a little bit out of control, they agreed to retreat back into the bush and lay low for a while. Eva suggested that they go along the route described by the native in his story about the rainbow snake and the wombat tribe. Captain Naskin had not the faintest idea what she was talking about, it all seemed reasonable, he was sure willing to comply, he did not wish an argument, he was just very eager that they should have sex again shortly.

They strode a short way further up the slight slope and then, having reached the extent of Captain Naskin's path they cleared the trees and rounded a crop of sharp rock and found themselves in a small clearing where the paper bark lay thick upon the ground, much like a mattress thought Captain Naskin, and here in this haunting and magical grotto, much to their surprise, they encountered...

...The Colony Astronomer (Chapter 44)

The Colony Astronomer was standing at the cliffside edge of the clearing, leaning against a tree and had his left arm clutched horizontally across his chest supporting the elbow of his right. His right forearm was perpendicular to his upper body which left his hand floating conveniently in the vicinity of his face and he alternated between chewing upon his fingernails and inhaling upon his tobacco and scratching upon his sideboards. His clothes upon him were filthy and rank, his eyes were bloodshot, his hands were shaking madly and there was ash and stain all about his person, in fact there was nothing about his appearance to suggest that this had been anything but a normal day for the Colony Astronomer. He was unaware of the arrival of the Spanish Girl and Captain Naskin and was looking down upon the mad and apocalyptic events unfolding in Old & New Bridgeford and was shaking his head and repeating to himself what to the Spanish Girl sounded like 'Folk, Folk, Folk' and he kept shaking his head despairingly. What Eva heard as 'Folk, Folk, Folk' was to the ear of Captain Naskin more akin to 'Fork, Fork, Fork'. It could have been either; it was in fact neither. He noticed them enter his clearing and immediately cleared both his thoughts and his throat and said,

'Oh, I'm sorry. I didn't think anyone else would... I've only *just* fled here.'

'There's no shame in that...we fled here too.' Said Eva.

'Well... I can flee elsewhere.'

'No you should stay with us.'

'Well if you two were off and on your way...'

'We were going to make contact with the Portuguese.'

'But what of the town?'

'There is no safety in this place any more, they are all about shooting each other and they have burnt down our house.'

'It is surely a strange affair.'

'We hope that the Portuguese will offer us sanctuary.'

'Well...if I could at the same time travel in the same direction towards the Portuguese...not necessarily with you but for safety's sake within the same vicinity.'

'You can come with us.' Said Eva.

'The Heavens be praised.' Said the Astronomer and then he said, 'Can I bring someone with me?'

'Good Lord we are not adverse to survivors indeed we welcome as many of them as can be mustered. What could have given you such a contrary opinion?'

'Can you allow me twenty minutes?'

'Take thirty. Good luck. Give this man your pistol, Ricardo, he is going to save a soul.'

And whilst Captain Naskin was overtook by a shiver of the third order the Colony Astronomer said,

'I already have about me a pistol.'

'I wouldn't take thirty.' Said Captain Naskin. 'Seeing as how those flames are fast taking to the upper branches. I'd say you've got ten...not even six.'

'Well then I'll...' Said the Colony Astronomer but his succeeding words were drowned out by an almighty great boom that exploded from the valley and they all turned to attend the bizarre spectacle that was unfolding below and before them.

CHAPTER 45 'BANG!!'

It was a wagon that had exploded. It was a wagon unattended by the side of the garrison stables. It was half loaded with a pile of fungi and toadstool and moss taken from the colony's swamps, this mound of mould was covered with dry branches and bark taken from the North fields. Who amongst them could have for a moment imagined the makeshift oven, the wild furnace these two profoundly disparate types of flora would create when thrown together in the back of a wagon? Who could have anticipated the wild and natural time bomb these two strange and unfamiliar plants were creating as they sat madly out of their accustomed environment and cooked against each other beneath the scalding afternoon sun? The one fermenting madly, the other crackling crisply. Why there are ponies next door. Who could have foreseen what would happen when a flame was set to the branches and the oil? No one really. It was a kind of soggy smell that hung around wetly.

The other half of the wagon was loaded with barrels of gunpowder and there should have been no person amongst them unsure of the results of setting fire to a wagon so loaded.

It blew the head off Convict Crosswell who did the lighting. It took the nuts off Convict Pakenham who did the urging, burnt each and every hair from the body of Corporal Peters hiding behind the jurist's table; it wrenched an eye from Forrester's face.

It diverted Captain Naskin, Eva the Spanish Girl and the Colony Astronomer.

CHAPTER 46

Our Bennelong did. And when Robertson woke up the next morning and noticed that all the other soldiers had abandoned him, read the note explaining why they had done so, left and scarpered in what they concluded was the best means of ensuring their own survival, and done so according to some bizarre and fiendish logic that made sense only in their own brains and required—for some reason—him not accompanying them—something about rank and chain of command—he tossed their letter away and, armed with the rememberings of his dream, he strode himself off along the chain of small saplings. Our Bennelong was right about that snake's poison spur, Robertson put a drop of the water to his lips and that was sufficient to have him vomiting. Stopping off in the belly was a festival, the food was terrific and some of the local folk even taught him that clever way of putting that fish gut upon his forehead, that fish gut that never boiled—God forbid that it should melt—and set the mosquitoes about other tasks. The last trip home was an ease such that he has since a thousand times traced that distance on map after map and more maps and concluded it an error of all the Cartographers.

He clomped, relieved, dazed and drunkenly down that hill to the Portuguese's beach like a Lancashire footman. When his calls of greeting commanded the attention of a few of the mustachioed Portuguese sailors he smiled at them beatifically and held his arms from his sides to indicate that he had forfeited his weaponry. When he gibbered on incomprehensibly to them, and kissed each new one of them he met, greeted their confused and befuddled eyes with his bright smile and his hearty hugs, when he said *'I do not speak your language. Can you find me an Englishman?'*, they took him to Eva and that filled his head with a thousand thoughts to consider but no brain to do so. He smiled at her in awe and wonder unable to speak a word, barely able to think one, and she returned his greeting with a look of pleasant surprise which was to Robertson's eyes fast replaced with a frown of concern and anxiety which was swiftly displaced by a look of alarm at his ruinous appearance.

If meeting up with the Spanish Girl here of all places, beside the Portuguese Caravel adocked in this bay, was indeed the stuff of wonderful dreams, then seeing her soon joined by a healthy looking and robust Captain Naskin who warmly stood by her side and gently petted her shoulder, a touch she tenderly leant towards and returned, was the stuff, yea the stuff, of hideous nightmares. He was in the middle of an exhaustion-induced and sun-stroke compelled, horrid nightmare, he would swear it.

He was horror-struck and horrified but somewhere in the back of his mind he recalled that even the most horrid nightmare carries with it that silent promise that at some point one will eventually awaken.

He will remember with fond nostalgia those days when this horrid nightmare of Captain Naskin and the Spanish Girl—so warm and fond with each other, he smiling and attentive, her, noticeably full around her dear belly, her breasts distinctly plump, and together with each other in the company of the Portuguese by their boat in the bay and so comfortably ensconced—was precisely that. A horrid nightmare. A filthy wretched ma-shaming dream and a bizarre and twisted rumination, something from which he could at some point wake up. Those golden days would be remembered dearly, they would seem a time of pleasure and plenty compared to those lean years that followed where Captain Naskin and Eva together as a happy couple became a cold hard reality.

They were salad days compared to the days that unfolded before him, fuck me yes. Naskin and Eva disappeared together back into the bush. They packed up camp, 'Thank You-ed' the Portuguese, bequeathed hearty handshakes for their generous Iberian hospitality, wished Young Robertson all the very best and disappeared into the bush and out from the pages of history, until civilisation pushed itself further into that wretched continent, the reach of the burgeoning colony of Old & New Bridgeford spread further and further inland, and eventually history unearthed them and discovered them the masters of a mighty farm. It considerably riled Young Robertson that when the Naskins reappeared to history they had forged themselves a kingdom, they had a lumber mill and a stable and a vegie patch, they had themselves a fenced-off field of sheep, a storehouse and a grainhouse, a kurrapuuk coop and a scallop farm and a yabbie dam, they had possum ramps and frog chunnels and around the back a blacksmith's humpy. They had a remarkable number of children.

Oh yes, it bugged him.

They proved themselves reliable and no-nonsense folks; they were charming and soon liked by all. The new colonists who had arrived over these many years all respected Captain Naskin, they were delighted to trade with him, they eagerly learnt the lessons this land and the natives had taught him. They loved his wife.

The new colonists knew nothing about Captain Naskin's inglorious past, when Young Robertson earnestly appraised them of the details, they were shocked and disbelieving, they would refute and rebut and rebuke him. They either punched him in the face or slapped him upon the face; it depended upon their gender.

The Naskins were trusted. She was always happy to trade two sacks of fur for a sack of sugar, he could be bargained up to fourteen bales of wool for a pouch of tobacco. They traded gold for everything the eye could see.

Young Robertson was disgusted to note the incredible change of character displayed by this new and radically improved Captain Naskin and yet he was unable to resist being charmed by this remarkable new fellow's wonderful company.

He noted the way in which Eva had bloomed with every day, had took upon herself the task of building a family and building a kingdom and had found herself glorystruck by that joy.

And whilst there might have been whispers that Naskin may have neglected his duties in a criminal manner, Captain Naskin and Eva shared out enough gold to ensure that they remained only whispers. He may have abandoned his post at a time of duty, but it was well understood that at the time, it was not much of a post to abandon.

Robertson tallied up the number of their progeny, calculated their ages and gestation period, and couldn't help but speculate upon the short period of time this couple allowed between birth and procreation, and consequently, the frequency with which they enjoyed conjugal relations. That dismayed him.

It was woe laid upon woe for poor old Robertson those days where the story of Captain Naskin and Eva unfolded before his eyes. When these stories revealed the times that Naskin and Eva had shared and forged together they filled his heart with bile and compelled his disgust, the idea of those two together boldly battling up a life and a livelihood and a stake and a claim and such a large family it repulsed and disgusted him and I'm sorry but I cannot help but wholeheartedly disagree with him.

I think it the happiest union my pen could write.

He should have let bygones be bygones.

There was some consolation for Young Robertson when he finally returned to Old & New Bridgeford after his six years of aimless journeying, after the wild adventures that had seen him frozen and starving in Quebec, that had seen him listless in Tahiti, a mercenary in Bolivia, and mishandled by pirates in the Flemish Passage, all awash in the Sea of Jutz. It enriched him this return to a place that if not England, at least had been a home. Of sorts. He was upset when he learnt how Naskin and the Spanish Girl had panned out, as I have explained above, but he was pleased when he discovered a long-lost parent.

The colony had a new Governor and that Governor was the sole and only present and there remaining survivor of that original party who had made that place their home. He discovered that the man governed the Colony of Old & New Bridgeford with a sure hand and an even hand and a very able hand. He also consequently discovered in a round about manner, and after long evenings of conversation shared with the gentleman, and a long time after the fact had been realised by the other fellow, that time spent in this gentleman's company was in fact, time spent in the company of his father.

That whilst he had not found a wife in this land across the world, he had found his Da. When he discovered this fact he was sure willing to co-operate with that gentleman's ruse.

Chapter 47

Which basically leaves us with just the cannibals to attend to.

Right. When the cannibals finally set about rowing back to Old & New Bridgeford, after they had finished their feast of human flesh, cleaned themselves and scoured and purged themselves and vomited themselves empty, after they had remembered to pull and drag the corpse away and push it off into the ocean where it was fast devoured by sharks, and then cleansed and scoured and purged themselves and vomited themselves empty a second time, they did so with very heavy hearts. They took that trip in the rowboat with a fearful shame deep within their souls that each time it took their attention it threatened to overwhelm them, so they thought about the rowing and they thought about the waves and they thought about the pile of cobblestones out the back of their last home in England and they thought about anything but. John Dunnock found the trip no more agreeable than he had the first time.

As they neared Old & New Bridgeford they welcomed the routine and order that the place promised, confident that their story about the accidental death of Doctor Wilmot was agreed upon and their reasons for returning with the prisoner were well understood—noting that the place seemed to be a lot more smoky than it usually seemed to be—and holding in their heart the hope that the regimen and discipline that life in Old & New Bridgeford offered would distract them from their shame. They were eager for the stability and infamy that life in this land represented, eager to catch sight of the men with the whips and the men with the welts, eager to spy their fellows about their daily business of dealing violence and trading hate, impatient to return to this cluster of wretches planning their evil and brewing up and whipping up and creating their sin because they'd just caught sight of themselves in the midst of a sin of a whole new order. A sin of their own devising and a sin so dastardly that it would even compel the disgust of this nest of vermin, this nettle of infamy, and they wished to avoid thinking about that.

They were eager to return to the real world because when they'd just been alone and came up with their own world, it really scared them.

It played with their minds a tad that when they disembarked from that boat in the eerily quiet and fireswept colony they were not greeted by the order and common ritual of life in Old & New Bridgeford at all, no no, but of all things, were presented with a generous plain of well-cooked cadavers.

Ten little cannibals huddled cold and deranged in a field of flesh and feasted and fought and retched and made graves for their faeces. In the canopies of all manner of trees, they hid with ease from the Portuguese. They grew more and more frightened of each other. They picked each other off, sometimes in a spontaneous act of deranged fury, occasionally in a well-organised co-operative of vicious hunters. A few wandered off and died in the bush.

One survived. One who had more experience in fending for himself in this strange land, fending off its hand of madness, who had not only subdued its challenge, but had then, with his rocks and his lines and his words and his markings, imposed upon it his will.

THE END

Acknowledgements

The story of Qamar al-Zaman which appears on pages 172–173 is from *The Arabian Nights* and this version of the tale is from Husain Haddawy's excellent translation, *The Arabian Nights II: Sinbad and Other Popular Stories*, Norton, 1995.